Butterscotch Bliss
A Clean and Wholesome Sweet Second-Chance Christmas Romance
Cecelia Dowdy

Divine Desserts Publishing LLC

https://www. ceceliadowdy.com

Cover design silhouette image generated by Cecelia Dowdy Toomer via Midjourney Discord. Background and snow and house graphics provided by Canva.

ISBN - Paperback: 978-1-962537-03-2

First Edition: November 2024

Praise for Dowdy's Writing

D owdy writes with the right touch to keep the readers engaged and invested... - **USA Today**

Newsletter Signup

S ign up for my newsletter:

https://ceceliadowdy.com/sign-up-for-my-email-list/

https://www.bookbub.com/authors/cecelia-dowdy

Bookbub is a wonderful service that notifies you when books go on sale! If you follow me, you'll be notified about new releases and sales of my earlier titles!

Chapter 1

"Patrick, do you understand everything?"

Did he understand? Of course he did. His father looked directly at him, his blue eyes piercing him like lasers. This week was the first time he'd seen his dad in three years and instead of the friendly reunion that he'd imagined, his dad just wanted to talk about work.

"Patrick? Do you know what to do?" His dad asked the question slowly, as if Patrick were dimwitted. He mentally sighed. He'd been hired by his father one month ago. At the time he'd still been living in Ireland while his father continued to live in the states. He'd worked remotely for the first few weeks. Patrick had just returned to the Outer Banks two days ago, right after Thanksgiving, and he was already so tired of his father's, Roger Smith's, work ethic. Murmurings from staff members grumbling that Roger ran a tight ship and that work *always* came first. Well, maybe once he worked his way up to vice-president of finance for The Smith Shortbread Company his father would see him for who he truly was – his only son.

The pie chart on the computer screen glared like a neon sign. Going over the numbers, making comparisons, was time consuming, especially when he was performing the task with his dad. His dad's shortbread business had been thriving. The uptick in sales had made it possible for him to recently open up another factory on the outskirts of the Outer Banks. The business office was about a half hour from the cookie factory – right in the downtown area. In spite of their rocky relationship he felt a bit of pride whenever he spotted the Smith Shortbread lining the grocery store shelves.

"Patrick?"

Oh, right, he needed to respond to his father's question. "Yes, I understand." He'd need to work late for the next few days in order to be ready for the big meeting. He hoped that he'd have the mental and physical energy to do all that his dad had commanded. He glanced at his dad as he poured water into a glass. It'd seemed weird – having a meeting like this with just the two of them while sitting at the conference table. He'd wanted to meet with his dad in his office, but his father *never* held meetings in his office – even if the meeting was one on one. For the life of him, he didn't understand such a rule, so, he'd kept his thoughts to himself. Still a newbie, he figured he had to do what it took to move up the corporate ladder.

A long time ago, he recalled that his dad would sometimes forget small details. Well, he'd need to remind him about the impending weather. "What about the snowstorm?"

His dad glanced up from his laptop, already focusing on another task. The couple of meetings he'd had with his father had never adjourned. His dad would simply focus on a new task – giving the impression that he was finished with the discussion. "What about it?"

Patrick stood up and strolled to the large window in the conference room. Snow tumbled from the sky like fairy dust as people rushed down the sidewalk. The day had turned suddenly dark. Festive, colorful Christmas lights winked from the store windows.

"If it snows as much as predicted, we might have people unable to come to the office. How will you hold tomorrow's meeting?"

"It might not snow that much. If it does, we'll do it via Zoom or phone if we have to. No way am I cancelling this meeting because of some snow. You just be sure you have your profitability review done for the meeting." The profitability review was a deep dive into their current products which would prove their strong financial position – ensuring that The Smith Shortbread Company was ready for expansion. His father wanted to branch out and create a savory shortbread product. Such a product would be used as a pairing with sharp cheeses and cured meats. One of the marketing staff members envisioned the packaging for the new products would display a huge charcuterie board.

He continued staring out the window. Okay, looked like he needed to be more direct. He gestured toward the large picture windows. "It just started snowing."

His father jerked his head toward the window, his eyes widening. "Still might not snow as much as they said." His dad then closed his laptop. "Don't worry about the snow. Just be sure your work gets done. Be careful driving home." He then exited the room without saying goodbye.

Patrick shook his head. He honestly didn't understand why his dad's personality was the opposite of what he remembered when he was a boy. The camping and fishing trips he used to take with his dad while they lived in Ireland played in his mind constantly. The urge to grab those memories and push them forward to now – was what he wanted to do.

It appeared his father didn't see it that way. The last time he'd seen his father happy was when they'd gone on a father-son fishing trip. His dad was American and he'd told Patrick that he'd need to return to the states for a little while. The news had changed Patrick's life. At the time he'd been an only child and had enjoyed spending time with his dad. He'd only been eight years old and once his dad left, he'd not been the same. He'd visited the states and had seen his father each summer for a few weeks. However, the joy that they'd shared had quickly evaporated like steam rising from a hot cup of coffee. Each summer his dad had dated a new woman. Usually the lady had one or more children. He'd spent his summer vacations babysitting someone else's kids while his dad became enamored with his new girlfriend. He honestly didn't understand *why* it took his father so long to settle down. His dad had been married for three years now, but, Patrick just couldn't seem to get close to his dad's new family. He'd only met his step siblings once and hadn't felt the need to bond with them after that.

He gulped and fisted his hands. Anger again surged within him. He'd tried to reconnect with his dad over the years but the distance between them remained. He inwardly groaned. Well, no sense in dwelling on that. Maybe in due time, once he'd been promoted a few times, his father would be willing to start having a *real* relationship with him again. *Oh, Lord, I hope I didn't make a mistake in returning to the Outer Banks.*

Not only did he want to solidify his relationship with his father - he also wanted to apologize to Raquel Reese – his ex-girlfriend. He cringed, remembering their awful breakup over the phone. It'd been three years since that painful day. He slammed his laptop shut and shoved it into his backpack.

Since he'd just recently returned to town, Raquel probably didn't know that he was back. He needed to give her a heads up that he'd returned before she found out via their mutual friends.

He figured if she found out about his recent arrival from somebody else, she might get upset, wondering why he'd not reached out to her to tell her he was back. He closed his eyes. *Lord, please allow Raquel to be open to listening to me. I need to tell her what really happened. If it's Your will please help Raquel to forgive me. Amen.* He put on his coat and grabbed his backpack. He needed to make a quick trip to Butterscotch Bliss Coffee Shop to talk to Raquel.

Raquel flipped the sign on the door of her coffee shop, Butterscotch Bliss, from OPEN to CLOSED. Snowflakes tumbled from the dark sky as cars slowly passed by on the icy street. This was predicted to be one of the worse snowstorms in decades. She shivered. She doubted she'd be able to get an Uber in this nasty weather. She'd have to walk home. She had on her snow boots and her thick dark orange coat. Her house was only two miles away. The short distance provided a convenient reason for her to walk to work.

Loud music, followed by strong stomping, spilled from the upstairs apartment of her shop. Sounded like her assistant Brooke was exercising to a jazz exercise video. When Raquel had purchased her house, she'd allowed her assistant to move into the upstairs apartment. She glanced around her empty seating area. She carefully eyed each table. Her gaze swept over the pristine floor. Good, they'd not forgotten anything. No trash or empty coffee cups lying around. Normally, she'd box up the leftover Butterscotch Bliss Buns to take to the local soup kitchen. But not today. They'd sold out. She needed to make a double batch next time. Hopefully she'd be able to open the coffee shop tomorrow. Since it was snowing so hard, she wondered if she'd get many customers over the next few days. She dug her keys out of her purse and pushed the door open. A blast of frigid air spilled inside. Her face tingled from the cold. Just as she stepped onto the sidewalk, the door still open, the coffee shop's phone rang. She groaned. Not now. Maybe they'd leave a message. She'd take care of it tomorrow.

No, she'd better answer. One of her best and most difficult customers had placed a large special order earlier that day. She could imagine the woman was calling yet again to finalize more of her special demands. Fast as she could she rushed to the phone and answered it. "Butterscotch Bliss Coffee Shop."

Silence.

"Hello?" Perhaps the person who called hadn't heard her. She glanced at the caller ID. The long-distance number was unfamiliar. "May I help you?" She tried to recall if there were any other special orders that had been placed. It was possible that a customer was calling to cancel an order because of the snowstorm.

"Raquel? Raquel Reese?"

"Yes, this is Raquel. How can I help you?" She didn't recognize the slightly husky female voice.

"You don't know me. My name is Ama—" A loud noise, perhaps a cry, echoed through the phone.

She frowned as her heart skipped. Something was wrong. She could feel it. "Are you okay?" Maybe she needed to call the police or paramedics. Another sob resonated from the phone.

"I'm...sorry." The woman's voice wavered, as if it pained her to speak. "There's no easy way for me to tell you this."

"Who is this? Did you need some help?" Raquel gripped the phone. Dread filled her soul like an erupting volcano. Why would a stranger call her and start crying on the phone? It didn't make any sense.

"I'm Ama, your father's wife." She jerked back and frowned. This was obviously a mistake. This woman was distressed and had reached out to the wrong person.

She took a deep breath. All she needed to do was to explain to the caller that she had used the wrong number. Reese was a common last name. The woman was obviously trying to connect with somebody else. "I'm sorry...Ama. I'm afraid you've reached the wrong person."

"This is Raquel Reese, correct?" The woman's voice went up a few decibels as if she were getting ready to have an argument.

"Yes. I'm Raquel Reese, the owner of Butterscotch Bliss Coffee Shop on the Outer Banks. But I'm afraid you can't be looking for me. There must be some mistake."

"No mistake. Your father is Gregory Dennis Montague."

Her head buzzed as she took a deep breath. Maybe this was a prank. All she needed to do was hang up. But she couldn't. Her legs felt shaky, like jelly. She slowly walked to the nearest table and plopped onto the seat. "I don't have time for jokes." Her voice sounded funny. She almost felt as if she were a voyeur, staring at herself in the coffee shop, like a dream. Hey, that's probably the case. She had to be dreaming. Her momma once told her that if she ever wanted to figure out if she were dreaming to pinch herself. *"If you pinch yourself and you can't feel it, then you know you must be dreaming."* Her head felt so light that she didn't even have the energy to pinch herself.

She needed to get this woman off of her phone. Hey, wait a minute. She knew what happened. Perhaps this woman had been scammed. Maybe somebody had stolen her dad's identity. Was it possible to steal the identity of a dead person?

"Gregory Dennis Montague is your father, right. I'm his wife, Ama." The lady repeated the words slowly.

"But my dad's dead. He died when I was a baby." She needed to make this person understand that there was some kind of mix-up.

"No, he's alive." The woman sniffed. "You've got a birthmark on your lower back shaped like a butterfly. That's what your dad told me."

She squeezed the phone and closed her eyes. Absolutely nobody knew about that birthmark except her mom, close friends, medical doctors...and Patrick – the only man with whom she'd ever been intimate. Oh, how she hated the cherry-colored, slightly raised birthmark. Whenever she went to the beach, she made sure the mark was covered with her bathing suit.

The caller cleared her throat. A noise, like a sharp cry, cracked through the phone like thunder. *Lord, if I ever needed your help, it's now. Please help me to understand what's going on. This has to be some sort of prank.* "I'm sorry. This is a lot to tell you right now. We don't have much time. Your father is sick. Cancer. They don't expect him to live through the night. He wants you to come and see him before he dies."

"What?" Her hands shook so hard that the phone slipped and dropped on the floor. She quickly picked it back up. Her heart pounded like a sledgehammer. "That can't be."

"Honey, I'm sorry. It's true."

Tears slivered down her face. She tasted mucous on her upper lip. She grabbed a napkin from the dispenser on the table and wiped her face. She balled the napkin in her hand, holding onto it in a vice-like grip.

She could barely listen. As Ama continued speaking Raquel's breath caught. Blackness swirled around her like a swarm of angry birds. For the first time in her life, she thought she would faint.

Chapter 2

Patrick rushed down the snowy street. Raquel's shop was only a few blocks away from his dad's office. Hopefully he could catch her before she left. As he rounded the corner his heart lifted when he spotted the light spilling out of Butterscotch Bliss. Good. Somebody was still there. He slipped on an icy patch. "Ugh." His loud cry ripped through the snowy street as he slammed into Raquel's glass door. "Ugh." He rubbed his head and stood up. He swiped the snow away from the glass as he spotted Raquel. She slumped on the table. Lord, have mercy. He pushed the door open. Thankfully it wasn't locked.

"Hello? Anybody there?" A voice echoed from the receiver from the cordless phone. Looked like Raquel had dropped it. Ignoring the phone, he pulled Raquel into his arms. He touched her chest. Her heart pounded as she slowly opened her eyes.

"Patrick?" Her voice sounded slurred.

"Honey, what's wrong? We need to get you to the hospital."

"Hello? Hello?" That blasted voice again echoed from the phone. Raquel cried.

"Baby, what's wrong?" He stroked her face. It almost felt like they'd never broken up. It was just as it was when they'd been dating three years ago. She pointed to the phone.

He picked it up. "Who is this?"

"Who's this? Where's Raquel?"

She looked so frightened. Tears streamed from her eyes. "Patrick. My dad..."

"Baby, just take a deep breath." Raquel rarely mentioned her father. She'd never had a relationship with him since he died when she was a baby. Strange that she'd speak of him now...he was obviously missing something.

"Who is this?" Again, the voice on the phone. Well, he needed to take charge. Whoever this was, the phone call had upset Raquel. She looked like she was in shock.

"Hi, Raquel isn't well." He glanced at the display on the phone. He recited the number. "Can we call you back when she's feeling better?"

"Yes. You must hurry though. Not much time. He's not expected to live through the night." The woman sighed. "You must come now before it's too late." The stranger ended the call.

Ten minutes later Raquel warmed her hands on the mug of hot chocolate that Patrick had kindly provided. The music from Brooke's exercise video boomed from the upstairs apartment, so she'd likely not heard anything downstairs. As she'd sipped her rich, hot drink she'd had to get over her shock of suddenly seeing Patrick, in the flesh, for the first time in three years. He looked good – his pale skin, deep emerald-colored eyes, and thick red hair had made her swoon with pleasure years ago. She'd not been saved when they were dating, so, their relationship had been intimate. With vivid clarity, she recalled the times she used to spend in his apartment.

Now he was here, with her, during one of the most shocking moments in her life. Could God have had a hand in Patrick's presence here, right now? She took another sip of the hot chocolate. The drink tasted warm and sweet, kind of like the kisses she used to share with Patrick. She pushed the unwelcome thoughts away. Not wanting to think about the phone call she stared at Patrick, still trying to come to terms with his presence. "What are you doing here?"

"My dad recently relocated the corporate office for The Smith Shortbread Company to the Outer Banks. He hired me to work for him. I wanted to tell you that I'd moved back before you heard it from somebody else."

She set down her drink. "You're working for your dad?" She knew how much he lamented about not having a close relationship with his father since he'd been a boy.

"Aye. But, don't want to talk about that now. What was that all about on the phone?"

She told Patrick about the phone call that she'd received. "At first I thought it was a prank call, but, when she mentioned the birthmark…Patrick, she knew stuff about me that a stranger wouldn't know. It's such a shock to hear that my dad might be alive."

He raised his thick red eyebrows. "Shocking that she knew about the birthmark."

"Yeah. It's kind of spooky." She noticed the bruise on his forehead. "What happened?" She reached over and touched the bruise. He winced.

"I slipped on some ice and banged my head on your door. Lucky your door didn't break. My head hurts now. You have any Tylenol?" She nodded toward the counter. "My purse is back there." He returned minutes later with her purse. She opened it and gave him some pills. He borrowed her cup of cocoa and took a few sips to swallow the tablets. "So, Rocky, do you believe this woman? What's her name? Ama?" Rocky. Oh, how she'd missed his rich Irish brogue when he used to speak her nickname – a nickname that he'd made just for her.

She swallowed a sip of cocoa before taking a deep breath. "I feel like I should believe her. I'm so shocked. I don't know what to do."

"Let's call her back." After he placed the call, Raquel put it on speaker. The familiar female voice answered.

"This is Ama."

"Hi, it's Raquel. Look Ama, this is a shock to me. I was having doubts about what you told me."

"Raquel, I understand. I tried to convince your father to reach out to you over the years, but, he wouldn't do it. He said he was ashamed."

"Ashamed of what? Why would my mom lie to me for my entire life? She told me that my father was dead."

"I can't speak about your mom's actions." She whimpered. "I'm sorry. I'm just upset since Greg's so sick. You must come." Ama remained silent for a few seconds. "We're in Royal Spring Hospice Center in Royal Spring Pennsylvania. He really wants to see you. It would mean so much to him."

Patrick took her hand. The warmth of his touch soothed her. "Ama, my name's Patrick. I'm a friend of Rocky's."

"Rocky?" Ama sounded confused.

"I'm sorry. I'm Raquel's friend. There's a massive snowstorm over the entire Mid-Atlantic."

"Yes, I know. It's bad over here too. I know it's a terrible time to travel, but, I wouldn't ask if Greg didn't think it was so important."

"Can we do a Facetime or Zoom call or something?" Patrick suggested.

"He's not conscious right now. He's been in and out of consciousness over the last twenty-four hours." She sighed. "If you can't make it, we can try a Facetime when he wakes up, but I can't guarantee when, or if, that'll happen." She took a deep breath. "I think he will wake up if he knows that Raquel is here."

Patrick eyed the phone. "Ama, we'll text you when we're on our way. We'll keep you posted during the trip."

As he ended the call, Raquel gripped the handle of her mug. "You can't just make a decision like that before discussing it with me."

"Ah, Rocky. I know you. You'll be upset. It'll eat away at you if you don't go. I can't say that I understand how you feel right now, but, I just know that we need to make the effort to go." She finished her mug of chocolate, realizing that the warmth from the hot drink soothed her frazzled nerves. Patrick continued holding her hand. Her mocha brown skin contrasted with his pale whjte complexion. He caressed her fingers. "I probably should've asked you this beforehand."

"What?"

"You're not seeing anybody are you? I shouldn't be sitting here holding your hand and helping you if it's going to make somebody angry."

She shook her head causing her long dreadlocks to sway. "No, I'm not seeing anybody." It was a bit troubling that Patrick swooped in here when she felt so vulnerable. It felt too good and too easy to just slide back into their old routine – a routine that had abruptly ended three years ago. "Are you seeing someone?" Heaven help her if he were dating someone. She'd have pulled her hand away quickly and berated him for being so forward.

"Nah." He continued to hold her hand, caressing her skin. "Is it still the same as before?" His sexy voice interrupted her thoughts.

"What do you mean?"

"Driving. You don't drive. I assume that you still haven't learned?"

"I still don't drive. I only live a couple of miles away. I walk to and from work if the weather is good. Otherwise, I take an Uber." When they were dating Patrick had offered to teach her how to drive, but, she'd never taken him up on it.

"I have a new SUV. It's a four-wheel drive that handles snow. If we get started now, we can probably make it before morning." Having Patrick to take charge and make plans that weren't any of his business was beyond unnerving. Her head was still spinning with the fact that her father was alive – not dead as she'd been told her entire life. She had tons of unanswered questions. All she wanted to do was to get into bed and have a good night's sleep while she digested this new information.

But Patrick *knew* her. If her dad died before he had a chance to see her – and she'd not made the effort to go and visit him...well, it would eat away at her for a good long while. She knew she'd have a hard time forgiving herself for not making the effort to see her father.

"Rocky, you're upset." He continued holding her hand. "When I moved to Ireland to take care of my sisters after my mum died, I made some changes."

"What kind of changes?"

"I...how about we get going? I can tell you while we're on the road."

"It looks like you bumped your head pretty hard on my door. Are you okay to drive?"

"Aye. It'll be fine." Both of them stood up. "My car's a few blocks away. Won't take me long to take you to your place and you can get your stuff. I'll do the same. We'll be on the road in less than an hour."

She approached Brooke's upstairs apartment and heard the shower running. She quickly texted her assistant, letting her know that she'd be leaving for a few days and would be in touch. She encouraged her to open the shop the next day if she could. She doubted they'd have many customers if the storm was as bad as the weatherman had predicted.

Chapter 3

Patrick rushed into his apartment and grabbed his gym bag. He unzipped it and threw in a few changes of clothing. His heart pounded while his hands shook. He needed to calm down. He got down on his knees, steepled his hands. He kept his eyes open and stared up at the ceiling. For some reason, when he prayed alone, he'd always preferred *not* to close his eyes. He knew that God could see him and hear him, no matter how he chose to pray. But, when he looked up, his face toward the sky, he just felt closer to God, as if the Lord could see the distress and torment in his expression.

"Lord, I really need your help. I want to help Raquel, but, I don't want to let my dad down. He wants me to prepare my profitability review for tomorrow's meeting. I can't do that if I'm going to be driving all night." He closed his eyes for a few moments and recalled how happy his dad used to be, the closeness that they used to share. He sensed that the dad of his childhood would've understood *why* he needed to help Raquel. However, the dad of today would be upset if he wasn't ready for the presentation. The urge to reconnect with his dad rushed through him – almost like a raging inferno. He wanted his dad to like him and accept him so that they could reconnect and be close again, as close as when he was a child. *Tell him the truth.*

The words seemed to wash over him, calm and clear, like the cool water that rushed over the smooth dark rocks at the river near his home in Ireland. His dad needed to know the truth so he had to tell him. Opening his eyes, his hands still clasped, he stared at the smooth white ceiling. "Lord, please help me to say the right thing to my father. Amen."

Unclasping his hands, he plopped down on the bed and pulled his phone from his pocket. He accessed his father's number from his contacts. His heartbeat sped up as the phone rang. Once. Twice. Three times. His dad's firm strong voice boomed through the phone. When the beep sounded for him to leave a message he waited a few seconds. "It's Patrick. I have a friend who needs to travel tonight. It's life or death. She needs to see her dad before he dies. She can't find anybody else to take her during the snowstorm, so I must help her. I will be in contact and have my laptop with me. I promise to have the materials that you need for the meeting if you agree to reschedule. I feel bad about this, but, promise to make it up to you. Call me as soon as you can." He ended the message and slid the phone back into his pocket. He needed to hurry up and pack. Hopefully he'd be able to get Raquel to her father in time.

Patrick popped the last bite of the chicken salad sandwich into his mouth as he slowly drove down the snowy street. Raquel's chicken salad was so good, creamy and delicious. She'd made a huge batch of it to serve as lunch to her customers the following day. She'd taken half of it with them, along with a loaf of bread and chips, to eat while they were on the road.

He quickly eyed Raquel. Her seat was reclined all the way back and her eyes were closed. Shocking. He couldn't begin to imagine what she was going through right now or how she was feeling. Again, he thought about his dad and sighed. He supposed he needed to leave his negative feelings with the Lord and again ask Him to help. He wasn't sure if that was going to happen between him and his dad. His father had not called him back. With the snowstorm he was almost sure the office would be closed tomorrow. Maybe he should call him back. Well, maybe not. He'd wait until the morning before reaching out to his father again. Hopefully, he wouldn't be too upset.

He glanced at Rocky. At least he *had* a father. But, what was Rocky feeling right now? Why would her mom lie to her for her entire life, leading her to believe her father was dead? He inwardly groaned. *Lord, please don't let this be a wild goose chase.* He prayed that what Ama spoke was true. His gut told him that it probably was. Poor Rocky couldn't even confront her mother with this new information since her mom had passed away a year ago. *Lord, I'm still in love Rocky and--*

The ringing from his phone filled the car with an unwelcome noise, interrupting his prayer.

Raquel struggled to open her eyes. Patrick's SUV crept on the snowy road. He took the call...actually, it wasn't a regular call. It was a Facetime call. Two identical female pale faces with bright red hair smiled from the display. Patrick's half-sisters. Both of the girls were beautiful. She'd never met them in person, but, had spoken to them via phone when she'd dated Patrick.

"Hey Patrick." One of the girls chimed in. "We heard about the storm. You going to be okay?"

"Aye. Yes, it's been snowing. I'm driving now."

"In this weather?" The other twin frowned. "Are you sure that's wise?"

He tilted the phone toward her. "Say hi to Rocky. You remember her, right girls?"

"Oh, my goodness. You two are back together?" One of the twins asked the question.

Raquel's eyes widened. What had Patrick told them? Hopefully, he didn't give his sisters the wrong idea. She needed to make sure they understood that her and Patrick were not a couple. "Hi, girls. Nice to talk to you again. No, your brother and I are not together. It's a long story. He's helping me out with something. It would take me too long to explain."

Patrick eyed Raquel before focusing on the twins. "Bonnie, I want you to make sure you get your prescription filled for your medicine."

"Oh my God. Patrick. Don't say such personal stuff in front of Raquel. She doesn't want to hear about this."

He sighed. "Brenda, make sure you study for your exams next week. Don't be blowing off studying until the last minute. Bonnie, make sure your sister studies." He cleared his throat. "Both of you be careful. It's your first year at university and I know how wild young people can be when they're away from home for the first time."

One of the twins scoffed. "You're making a big deal out of nothing. We're fine."

He went on to talk about the soccer and hockey teams on which they played in college, reminding them to be careful when they played their sports. "Both of you don't forget to say your prayers every night before you go to sleep." He stopped talking. He gripped the steering wheel, his knuckles taut. Oh no. Looked like he was upset about something. "Take care. Bye." His voice softened as he ended the call.

"You worry about your sisters, don't you?" Her heart thundered with pride as he continued gripping the steering wheel as they slowly ambled down the snowy street.

"Aye. All the time. With my mum dying and all…hard on the girls."

What a huge commitment. He wasn't a big brother to Bonnie and Brenda – he was a father. When she'd dated him, she imagined having his children. She'd always sensed that he'd be an awesome dad. He'd been a volunteer coach for the local youth group. She fondly recalled how he'd worked with the young children when they played soccer in the fall, and track and field in the spring. She'd often spent time at the community center, watching him while he coached. His patient and caring nature had an amazing effect on the children. He'd been liked and well-respected when he'd lived in the Outer Banks.

But their happy glorious time together had been shattered like a broken Christmas light when his mom unexpectedly passed. Thinking about Patrick's father-like nature again made her think of her own father. She blew air through her lips. He reached over and patted her leg. The warmth from his brief touch made her feel good, a bit too good. Suddenly she realized that being alone with Patrick on a snowy road might be a bad idea. She was still so attracted to him. While she'd slept earlier, she'd dreamed about kissing him.

She pushed the thought away, again thinking about her dad. "I wish I knew more about why my mom didn't tell me the truth about my dad."

"Ah, Rocky. I figure this is hard for you. I wish there was something I could do to help you."

"But you are helping me. You dropped everything just to drive me to Royal Spring so I can see my dad before he dies." She swallowed.

Maybe she should stop stressing out about her father. She needed to focus on something else. "You mentioned that you'd made changes since you left and moved back to Ireland. What sort of changes were you talking about?"

"Rocky, after my mum passed, and I relocated back to Ireland, found a new job, and took care of my sisters. Well, it was rough. I'm not a dad." He'd returned to help raise his sisters since their biological father was not around. His mum had said the twins' father was no good and she'd divorced him years ago.

She touched his arm. "Don't be so hard on yourself. I'm sure you did the best that you could." From the brief Facetime call, it appeared that Bonnie and Brenda were happy.

"I had some help from people at the nearby church in Ireland. Do you know what I've been doing for the couple of hours that we've been driving?"

She shook her head. "I have no idea." She'd been so busy thinking, dozing off and on, that she'd not wondered what Patrick was doing.

"I've been praying. I openly accepted Christ after I started taking care of my sisters. Changed my entire life."

"Really?" She again thought about the time they used to spend together. She was about to respond about how wonderful it was that he'd accepted Jesus, when he reached over and grabbed her hand.

"I wanted to tell you something. Right before my mum passed, I'd wanted to let you know that I'd gotten saved."

Her eyes widened. "But you just said you got saved when you took care of your sisters."

"Aye. I openly made a proclamation after I started taking care of them. Right before that, I'd accepted Christ in my heart, privately." He took a deep breath. "I wanted to talk to you about it – tell you about my decision."

"I accepted Christ too. Not long after you left." She didn't mention how emotionally torn up, broken, and angry she'd felt. Melanie, one of her customers, as well as an acquaintance, had invited her to church. Accepting Christ had helped her to get through her breakup and move on with her life. When her mom passed last year, she'd also leaned on Him.

With clarity, she recalled their sudden broken date. "You broke our date because your mom died and you needed to go to Ireland."

"Aye."

"Then you broke up with me after that."

"Rocky. I'm so, so sorry."

Although they were no longer a couple, Patrick kept in touch with her by sending a Christmas card each year. He also had sent a huge floral arrangement when her mom had died the previous year. It was almost as if he'd broken up with her, but, had *not* wanted to do so. He dropped her hand and focused on the road. He was suddenly so quiet.

He was hiding something. She remembered how he'd get quiet when something was on his mind. At times, she felt he wanted to talk to her about something, but, wasn't sure *how* to tell her. When he'd get quiet like that, she'd gently ask if everything was okay.

He would usually confide in her. It just took him awhile to open up. Well, she wasn't going to push him. She was sure that he would tell her when he was ready.

The flashing lights of a police car caught her attention. Patrick expertly pulled over onto the side of the road. He lowered his window as the uniformed officer approached. "You have to get off of the road. The snowstorm is hampering traffic and only emergency vehicles are allowed out right now."

Patrick nodded. "Sure thing, officer." After he'd been given permission to leave, Raquel touched his arm.

"What if we don't make it in time? What if my dad dies—"

"Baby, don't think like that. Let's have some faith." Easy for him to say that. His father hadn't been predicted to die before the morning. "Can you call Ama? I don't think we're allowed to keep driving."

She called Ama's number. The call went straight to voicemail. "That's weird. She was so anxious for me to come, and now she's not answering her phone."

"Maybe her phone needs to be recharged. She's got a lot on her mind with her husband in hospice."

Sounded reasonable. She called Ama again and left a voicemail, explaining their situation. She then took a few deep breaths to calm herself down. She eyed Patrick. No question about it, she enjoyed having him here. Actually, she enjoyed his company a bit too much. His accented deep voice, good looks, and caring nature were like a healing balm on her shattered soul. She certainly needed his soothing kindness, but, heaven help her, there was no way she could spend the night with Patrick in a hotel. The thought gave her shivers. She was just too weak to resist the temptation. Maybe they could find two hotel rooms.

"Patrick." Her voice thundered in the car like a cannon. Why hadn't she thought of this before?

"Rocky, what's wrong?" He seemed concerned as he glanced over at her.

During this road trip, she'd been thinking about her father and her past relationship with Patrick, that she'd forgotten that they were now passing through the area which wasn't far from her cousin Frank.

"My cousin Frank lives on a farm a few miles from here." She glanced at the GPS to make sure it was accurate. "We can stay with them."

"Them?" Patrick had never met her cousin, so she needed to fill him in.

"His wife's name is Emily. They've been married for years. They have two kids. We can stay with them." She had not seen her cousin in a while. She pulled out her phone and called Frank. The call went straight to voicemail. She quickly plugged Frank's address into the GPS so that Patrick could continue their trip. "Let's go. Even with the snowy roads, we should be there in less than a half hour."

"Sure thing." Patrick rounded the corner and followed the instructions given by the GPS.

Chapter 4

Raquel and Patrick trudged through the snow as they approached the large ranch-style home. Her cousin's farm was a white expanse of beauty amid the darkness. Cows bellowed in the distance. Raquel sniffed. The farm stench wasn't so bad during the winter. The fresh clean scent of snow infused the air, almost making her forget about her problems. "It's so pretty out here." She stopped walking and just stared. If she didn't have so much on her mind, she could imagine just sitting on the porch with a hot cup of cocoa and staring at the white expanse in the inky darkness.

"Aye. It's nice to look at."

She opened the door of the screened-in porch. A brown and black medium-sized dog trotted over to them. "Hi, Cocoa, do you remember me?" She ruffled the dog's fur. It'd been a few years since she'd visited Frank and Emily's farm. The last time she'd seen them, Cocoa had just been a puppy.

"Hiya Cocoa." Patrick followed her example and stroked the dog's fur. She rapped on the door. The porch light came on. She glanced at Patrick. White flakes of snow clung to his red eyelashes. She squeezed her fingers into a fist, resisting the urge to brush the snow away from his eyes.

The door opened. Bright light spilled onto the porch.

"May I help…" Frank's mouth dropped open. "Raquel?" Her cousin's bald brown head shined beneath the bright light. Emily had confided that Frank had started going bald a couple of years ago and had felt self-conscious about it. That's when he started to shave his hair. He finally smiled, his hairless head was complemented by a full mustache and beard.

She hugged her cousin as hard as she could. "Oh, Frank, so much as happened." Her voice wavered.

"Whoa, glad to see you, too." She released him and he peered at her. "What's wrong? Your eyes are red. Looks like you've been crying."

"Frank, my dad—" Cocoa barked and tried to come inside. The dog wagged his tail. Looked like he was excited about their unexpected visitors.

"Cocoa, stay outside." His stern loud voice cracked through the cold night air like a whip. The dog whimpered and sulked into a corner.

"Poor Cocoa." She wished Frank would let the dog come inside. It was so cold her lips were numb.

Frank gestured toward the ample-sized doghouse on the porch. "He'll be fine. His kennel is insulated and has a heated bed. If it gets too cold we'll bring him in."

"Frank, who is it?" Frank's wife Emily came to the door. Her thick dark brown hair was gathered into a sloppy knot on the top of her head. A few freckles dotted the light brown skin of her face. The attractive woman grinned as soon as she recognized Raquel. "Raquel? What on earth are you doing visiting in the middle of a snowstorm?"

Before she could respond Emily hugged her hard. "It's so good to see you."

She returned Emily's hug. Their fourteen-year-old twins, Franklin Jr., who they called Buddy, and Judith, ran to the door and hugged Raquel. She couldn't believe how tall the twins had gotten. Both of the kids wore glasses. Since the door was still open Cocoa ignored Frank's warning and sprinted inside. Frank ignored the dog as he beckoned them into the house. "Come on in."

Patrick patiently followed Raquel into the house. She grabbed Patrick's hand. The scent of cinnamon and sugar seeped through the kitchen. Emily had probably been making Christmas cookies. "Everyone, this is my friend Patrick."

Frank shook Patrick's hand. "Pleased to meet you."

Emily hugged Patrick. "Any friend of Raquel's is a friend of mine. I'm so glad to meet you."

Patrick nodded toward Emily and Frank. "Likewise. Thank you."

Raquel gestured toward the twins. "This is Buddy and Judith."

Judith's eyes sparkled as she focused on Patrick and Raquel. "Aunt Raquel, we don't have school tomorrow because of the storm." Even though Raquel was their dad's cousin, not their aunt, they still insisted on calling her Aunt Raquel as a form of respect.

Buddy, nodded. "And you know what that means. No school means more time to play—"

"Video games." Both of the kids yelled the words simultaneously as they gave each other a high five.

The twins shared a strong resemblance to Emily. But, she could see some resemblance to Frank as well, especially the way Buddy tilted his head and bit his lower lip. Frank always did this when he was excited or trying to figure something out. Cocoa barked and wagged his tail, obviously excited about their impromptu guests.

Patrick eyed Emily as she cleaned up the kitchen after their im-promptu meal. She'd served them big bowls of leftover beef stew which she'd heated in the microwave. The cinnamon cookies they'd had for dessert had been amazing. Unable to resist, he snatched an-other cookie from the cookie jar and took a large bite. The strong taste of spicy cinnamon, sweet sugar, and melt-in-your mouth crunch exploded on his tongue. He moaned and took another bite. "These are the best cookies I've had in years."

Emily chuckled as she rinsed off another dish. He'd offered to help her with the dishes but she'd not accepted. "Judith made those. She's really interested in baking. She told me she wants to own her own bakery some day."

"Well, she's off to a good start." He finished his cookie and took a sip of decaffeinated coffee.

Raquel and Frank's voices drifted from Frank's office into the kitchen. He'd wanted to go in there with her while she explained to Frank what had happened the last few hours. But, she'd told him that she wanted to speak to Frank alone. He figured since Raquel wanted to find out if Frank, or perhaps other family members knew that her father was alive they might reveal why they'd not shared this information with her. Maybe she felt this was a family matter. If she found out any information Patrick was sure she'd share it with him later.

Emily was not a part of the conversation either. He figured Frank would tell Emily about his conversation with Raquel later. Far as he knew, married couples usually shared important information with each other.

"There. All done." Emily washed the last dish and placed it into the rack. She joined Patrick at the table with a cup of coffee. The twins yelled from the family room, obviously excited about their video game.

"They spend a lot of time playing video games?" He knew that some kids played so much that they didn't participate in other activities and ended up gaining weight and having health problems.

She emphatically shook her head. "We have to limit their time in front of the TV. The only reason they're playing right now and are not in bed is because there's no school tomorrow. Both of them are involved in sports and they help out on the farm during the summer."

He nodded. That was good to know. The twins again shrieked with excitement. Unable to resist he glanced into the living room. "Mind if I go and join them?"

"You play video games?" She grinned as she asked the question.

"Sometimes. While I dated Raquel a few years ago I used to volunteer at a community center with the youth. I learned to play a few games."

He entered the living room. Both kids were so enthralled at the game that they seemed barely conscious that he was there. "Whoop!" Their game ended.

"Mind if I play?" At first both glanced at each other. Uh oh. Looked like neither one of them wanted to give up their game controller. "I'll only do a short game. I'm lousy at it."

Judith slowly gave him her controller. After they'd chosen a game he cleared his throat. "Uh, how do you play this game?"

The twins looked mortified and he laughed. "Don't worry. I can play." Soon his character scaled walls while dodging flying objects.

Buddy shrieked. "I'm gonna crush you, man."

"No way."

He played with the twins for a solid hour. He played so hard that his fingers started to get sore. "One more game." He didn't think he could handle any more excitement. The adrenaline rushed through his veins like liquid candy. He'd forgotten just how much fun he used to have hanging out with young people. Sure, he'd had fun with his sisters but he'd been a parent to them as well. Plus, his sisters had not enjoyed video games at all.

Patrick's character scaled the last wall. He dropped the controller and stood up and whooped. "I won."

The threesome shared high fives before the lights went out and the house became completely dark.

Frank, Raquel, and Emily entered the living room. The flashlight on Frank's phone splashed against the dark walls. "I'm going to go and find the candles and matches."

Emily touched his shoulder. "Don't forget about the oil lamps in the basement."

The twins grumbled and plopped onto the couch. Looked like it was going to be a long night.

Chapter 5

"Mom, wake up. I have to talk to you." Her mom sprawled on the bed fast asleep. Her deep snores filled the room. Her mother had always been a loud sleeper. Sometimes, she could hear her snoring all the way downstairs. "Mom." Raquel's loud voice echoed in the room. Again, she shook her mom's shoulder. Maybe if she rattled her hard enough, she'd wake up and give her some answers. Her mom finally opened her eyes. But, her eyes looked strange. Kind of glassy, as if she were on drugs. "Why do your eyes look like that?" Something was wrong but she couldn't focus on that right now. She needed to determine why her mom had never told her the truth about her father.

Her mother didn't say anything. She simply stared out the window. Appeared as if she were in a trance. Why was she acting like this?

"Mom, I have to talk to you. Why did you lie about my dad? Why didn't you tell me that he was alive?"

Her mom slowly turned her head toward Raquel. Her dry cracked lips contrasted with her smooth brown complexion. "Don't cry baby."

Her voice was so low that Raquel struggled to listen. She raised her hand toward Raquel's face. "Don't cry…"

"Stop it already. Answer my question." Couldn't her mom understand *why* she wanted to know about her father? Besides she wasn't crying. She was just upset and wanted her mom to tell her the truth.

Her mom's smooth brown hand suddenly became wrinkled. "Can't answer your question. Don't cry—"

The loud boom shook the house and rattled the windows. Raquel jerked awake as Cocoa scampered onto the couch, whimpering. She peeked out the window. Lightning slithered across the angry sky. Thundersnow. While she and Patrick had been traveling, they'd heard the weather report. The weatherman had predicted bouts of thundersnow. Surprising that such a loud noise didn't wake up the entire house. Patrick had always been a deep sleeper. No surprise that he didn't wake up.

She took a deep breath while stroking Cocoa's brown fur. The vivid dream of her mom clouded her brain. She sniffed as wet tears streamed from her eyes. Cocoa snuggled closer to her face and whimpered before licking her tears away. She hugged the dog. *Lord, what did my dream mean?* Still cuddling Cocoa she snuggled beneath the comforter. Cocoa whimpered before scampering back to his place near the fire.

Orange sparks from the fireplace lit the inky darkness of the room. She pulled the blanket over her head. Buddy and Judith slumbered in front of the fireplace nestled beneath their sleeping bags. Emily and Frank were in their bedroom with a battery-operated heater. Patrick had taken the guest room. She figured he'd need as much sleep as possible before they hit the road again – he needed to sleep in a bed instead of the sofa. The soft snores from Cocoa filled the room. She just couldn't sleep anymore. She'd been tossing and turning on the small sofa all night. Intermittent sparks of fire shot through the fire-place, creating a warm snuggly glow. She eyed the battery-operated clock on the wall. Two thirty. The inky darkness of the room haunted and invigorated her at the same time.

Well, since she couldn't sleep, she may as well *do* something. She rolled out of the warmth of the blankets still thinking about the dream she'd just had. She was probably so desperate to find information about her father that she was imagining what would have happened if her mom were still alive? Would her mother have felt remorse for not being honest?

She went into the bathroom and turned on the spigot. Her conversation with Frank the previous evening had not turned up any fruitful information. Frank said that all that he knew was that her dad had passed away. He'd offered to call his mom to see if she knew anything. Frank's mom and her mom were sisters. Then the lights went out and the phone lines were down as well.

Well, she needed to be patient and hope and pray that they were able to leave soon. The frigid cold water slapped against her hands like droplets of ice. Her lips shivered with cold as she washed up best as she could. She imagined the hot water heater wasn't working since they had no electricity. Still shivering she entered the dark kitchen. Frank had mentioned where they kept the flashlights and candles. After turning on the flashlight and lighting a few candles, she opened the refrigerator. Voila! Emily still kept her sourdough starter in the back of her refrigerator. She removed the starter and fed it with some flour, sugar and water. She found packets of yeast in the back of the fridge. Oh, no, she'd need warm water to make the yeast rise. She measured the water into a small pot and placed some oven mitts over her hands.

She then held the pot over the fire for a couple of minutes to heat the water. After she'd mixed her dough using her warmed water, she placed the lump of dough into a bowl and set it near the fire so that it could rise. No longer tired, she covered herself with a blanket and sat near the fire to watch the dough rise. Angst, as thick as pea soup, enveloped her. She dealt with her feelings the best way she knew how.

She prayed. She closed her eyes. *Lord, please help me. I'm fearful and joyous to discover that my dad is alive and that he wants to see me.* She continued talking to Jesus about her fear and joy about discovering that her dad, whom she thought was dead, was actually alive. She told Him about her reawakened feelings for Patrick. Being around him made her heart skip with joy – and with fear. Should she really open herself up and allow herself to be involved with him again? She opened her eyes. She'd been talking to God for over an hour. She still felt angsty and confused, but, she felt a bit better now that she'd confided in God. "Jesus, please help me." She mumbled the words aloud as she peered at the dough. It had risen quite nicely.

Still wide awake, she took the dough into the kitchen and measured the ingredients for her butterscotch sauce into a pan. Doing the same as she did with the dough, she took the pan and held it over the fire so that the ingredients could melt. She held it over the fire for a few minutes and then removed it and stirred it. She couldn't get the sauce as smooth as she wanted it, so this would have to do. She prepared her Butterscotch Bliss Buns and set them near the fire for a second rising.

She found eggs and bacon in the fridge. Emily usually collected eggs from their chickens each morning. She couldn't recall if the chickens laid many eggs during the winter months. She'd been out to visit Frank and Emily a lot of times over the years. Since the electricity was out she couldn't use the oven or any of the other kitchen gadgets. She recalled that Frank kept a charcoal grill in the shed. Putting on her coat and boots, hat and gloves, she stepped outside into the frigid cold, holding the flashlight. The snow was at least two feet deep, but the shed was only a few feet away. Snow tumbled from the sky and her lips shivered from the icy cold. She trudged through the snow. She opened the shed and chuckled as soon as she spotted the grill. Joy, as fresh as fallen snow, suddenly enveloped her.

Cooking always made her feel happy. About an hour later, the barbeque grill had been lit using the bag of charcoal that she'd found in the shed. She'd brought all of the food outside. *Lord, please let this work.* She'd never cooked her Butterscotch Bliss Buns over an open fire. Hopefully everything would turn out well. She'd watched a Youtube video about cooking bread over a barbeque grill a few months ago. Recalling the instructions on the video, she waited until the charcoal had turned white and placed the aluminum-foil covered pan of buns onto the grill. If she did this properly, they should be done within the next half hour. Using Emily's iron skillet, she fried bacon. The shed was cold, but with her thick boots and warm jacket, and sitting close to the grill, she kept fairly warm. The wind howled and some flakes of snow flew into the shed since she kept the door cracked so that the smoke from the barbeque grill could escape. She was pulling the bacon off of the grill just as the door cracked open.

Emily strolled into the shed holding a large plastic bag. Bundled in her coat and boots and with her face covered with a scarf, she looked ready to battle any snowstorm. "Raquel, have you lost your mind?" She pulled her scarf away from her face. Her light brown cheeks reddened with cold.

She shrugged as she finished preparing breakfast. "I couldn't sleep. Since the electricity is off I thought I'd make breakfast on your barbeque grill." Emily glanced at the food and grinned. She recalled how Emily would milk the cows each morning and when she returned to her house, she'd always worked up an appetite. "Did you milk the cows this morning?"

She nodded. "I got the kids up to help me. We had to milk them by hand since the milking machine is not working since the electricity is off." Emily's stomach then rumbled loudly with hunger.

Raquel laughed. It felt good, pleasant, to laugh about something after all she'd gone through the last twenty-four hours. "I've got Butterscotch Bliss Buns, coffee, eggs, bacon..." she paused. "The food will get cold if we take it inside. Why doesn't everybody come out here to eat? I can make an extra pot of coffee and put it in a thermos for us to drink later if you'd like." Emily left the plastic bag in the corner of the shed.

"I'll go in and tell everybody to come out here and eat."

Raquel gestured toward the plastic bag that Emily had brought in. "What's in that bag?"

Emily grinned. "An early Christmas present for you. No peeking. I wanted to talk to you about it and give it to you before you leave." She hesitated. "It's a personal gift. I want to be alone when I give it to you."

Raquel didn't think she could wait. Her curiosity bloomed within her like a newly sprouted flower. She eyed the sack as Emily scampered back into the house. Later she returned with everyone. They'd brought plates, cutlery and cups. Patrick came into the shed as everybody sat down to eat. His eyes, vivid as emeralds, looked sad. Oh no, he was worried...probably about her. He grabbed her into a hug and kissed her cheek. "Ya had me worried. I woke up and didn't see you. I was about to go look for you when Emily came in and told me that you were in the shed cooking breakfast."

"I'm sorry. I probably should've left you a note."

"Don't apologize, I realize you got a lot on your mind."

They sat in plastic lawn chairs and gobbled down the breakfast she'd fixed. She took a huge bite of the bun. Warm sweetness coated her mouth like a heavenly cloud. The buns tasted so good after being cooked on an open fire. The fluffy scrambled eggs paired nicely with the buns. She bit into the bacon, relishing the crispy salty meat. After she'd eaten her amazing meal, she sighed. She grinned when spotted that everybody's plate was empty. She glanced at the twins. "Did you two get enough to eat?"

The twins nodded. "It was delicious Aunt Raquel. Tasted better than mom's." Buddy's voice echoed in the small shed. Emily playfully swatted her son's shoulder.

Her head suddenly felt light, as if cotton were stuffed up her brain. Raquel stood up slowly. Her head buzzed. She squeezed her eyes shut.

"Baby, what's wrong?" Patrick's deep voice sounded far away, almost as if he were speaking to her from another room. The wind suddenly howled as snowflakes drifted into the shed. Darkness, thick as a nighttime sky, crowded her vision. She blinked before she passed out.

Chapter 6

"Raquel." Patrick's voice echoed in the shed as he pulled Raquel into his arms. Frank scampered over to Patrick. "Frank, she's fainted." His heart thrummed so hard, he felt it would pop out of his chest. Raquel had always been a worrier and hard worker. Sometimes, she had a hard time knowing when to stop. In the time he'd dated her, he'd never known her to push herself so hard that she'd faint.

Emily joined them. They'd sent the kids to the house to check to see if the landline was still down. Emily felt Raquel's forehead and checked that she was still breathing.

"The phone is still down, Dad," Judith returned to the shed to inform them.

Frank clapped Patrick's shoulder. "The roads are still not plowed. I'm going over to my neighbor's house. She's a nurse. Maybe she can come and check on Raquel."

Patrick barely nodded. "Thanks."

Lord, help us. Please let Raquel be okay. Amen.

Warmth, as strong and vivid as the hottest sun, wrapped Raquel like a comfortable snuggly blanket. She slowly opened her eyes. Covered with a thick quilt, she eyed the fire burning in the fireplace. She moaned as an unfamiliar woman bended over her. "Ahh. So glad you're awake."

The woman had pale skin and tight curly hair. "What happened?" Her mouth felt dry, like cotton, and she still felt lightheaded.

"You fainted. I'm Pauline, Frank and Emily's neighbor. I'm a nurse. When you fainted they wanted me to check on you. I think you just need to get some rest. You're stressed. Your boyfriend told me that you've been going through a lot lately."

Patrick was soon beside her and he took her hand. "Pauline said you're overdoing it. She said you should probably see a doctor and get a sedative."

She groaned. She didn't want to see a doctor. "Are the phone lines still down?" She still needed to see her dad before it was too late. What if he died before she arrived to see him?

"Baby, stop worrying. You're making yourself sick."

Pauline nodded. "Listen to him. You need to calm down. Emily has some lavender pills. You might want to take some to help you to relax. I think after you've had a good night's sleep, you'll be okay. But, just to be sure, you need to see a doctor before you continue your trip."

No way was she wasting precious time to see a doctor. Emily came into the room with a small packet. "These are the lavender pills. I take them when I have trouble sleeping. You might want to take one now and try and get some sleep. You and Patrick won't be able to leave yet since the roads still haven't been plowed."

"I don't want to go to sleep now. What if the roads get cleared and the cell phone service is back up? I need to be awake for that."

"Raquel." Patrick's sexy mouth mashed down in anger as he glared at her. "I will wake you up if anything happens. We're worried about you. You're so hard-headed that it's making you sick. I know you want to see your dad. We'll do everything we can to make it happen."

Oh no, she'd upset Patrick. He was worried about her. She supposed her actions didn't help matters much. She just couldn't control all of the worrying she'd gone through the last couple of days.

Pauline nodded from across the room. She pulled her boots onto her feet and bundled up in her thick coat. "As a medical professional, I can vouch for what Patrick is saying. Remember what I said about seeing a doctor." Emily and Frank walked Pauline to the door. They spoke in hushed whispers as Raquel stared into Patrick's mesmerizing green eyes.

"I'm sorry, Patrick." Her voice was barely a whisper.

"Ah, Rocky. I know you're sorry. I just wish there was something I could say or do to make you feel better."

He'd done nothing but help her since he'd found out about her dad. As he held her hand, she was again reminded about those old feelings that were being rekindled. The warmth and familiarity of being around Patrick made her feel a bit skittish, glad, and scared at the same time. Her feelings for Patrick and hearing the earth-shattering truth about her dad – both of those things thundered within her. She squeezed Patrick's hand. "Oh, Rocky." His deep voice filled with distress as he handed her a tissue.

That's when she realized she was crying. The salty wetness slid down her cheeks. She just needed to relax and calm down. Shameful to be bawling like a baby. She needed to be strong as they waited for this snowstorm to be over so that they could get on the road.

The front door slammed shut as Pauline left. Frank went upstairs as Emily approached them. "Patrick, is it okay if I speak with Raquel alone?"

Patrick opened his mouth, as if he were about to say something. He glanced down at Raquel. *He doesn't want to leave me.* The thought slammed right into her like a freight train. He was going to argue with Emily about leaving her. He was worried. Drat, she'd gone and made such a mess of things and all he wanted to do was help her. Well, she would do what she needed to do to ensure that Patrick stopped worrying. *Lord, please help me. I know that there's a reason why I'm just finding out that my dad is actually alive, and that Patrick has returned. I need your guidance right now Lord. Amen.*

First, she needed to make Patrick feel better. She realized she could overdo it and be stubborn at times. "I'll take one of Emily's lavender pills. I'll try and rest after I've spoken to her."

He squeezed her hand. "Promise?"

She nodded. "I promise."

Patrick hesitated before approaching Emily. They whispered for a minute before Patrick left the room.

He didn't want to leave Raquel alone right now. He started up the stairs and stopped. He took a good look at her. She looked fragile. He just wanted to hold her, kiss her, and guarantee that everything would be okay. *Lord, she's the most beautiful, most precious woman in the world.* Her smooth mocha brown skin reminded him of the rich hot chocolate she served in her coffee shop. Her dreadlocked hair, full lips, high cheekbones... Warm liquid heat enveloped him. He blew air through his lips as he made his way up the stairs. *Lord, hopefully she can forgive me when I tell her the truth about everything.*

Judith and Buddy sprawled on the floor in Buddy's room. Both of the kids scowled. They looked as if the world had come to an end. "Mind if I come in?"

Buddy shrugged. "Sure."

He plopped on the bed. "What're you two looking so sad about?" He'd think they'd be excited since school was out.

Judith pursed her lips. "Why do you think we're upset? We're mad because we can't play video games."

Was that all?

"Do something else."

The girl's eyes rounded as she sat up. "Like what? We can't *do* anything without cell phone service or electricity."

Well, he needed a project. Something to take his mind off Raquel. Judith and Buddy were upset. He determined that they would be in better spirits soon. "Why don't you read your Bible?" He was sure they had Bibles around the house somewhere.

Buddy chuckled. "Are you kidding? That's boring."

But it wasn't boring. They should realize that. "I'm sure you read your Bibles sometime."

Judith joined him on the bed. "Of course. When we look up scriptures in church. Sometimes we read stuff in Sunday school."

"Hmm. I have an idea. I noticed some of those video games you play feature superheroes."

Buddy plopped onto the bed. "Yeah, so?"

Well, they were fourteen. Old enough to read things as they were in the Old Testament. "You ever read about Samson in the book of Judges?"

Judith perked up. "Sure. We learned about him a long time ago in Sunday school. He wasn't very smart. Delilah made a fool out of him."

Well, that much was true. "The Lord granted him great strength through of his hair. You're bored and need something to do. Go get your Bibles and read Judges chapters 13-16." Surprisingly the twins left the room and returned with their Bibles without complaining. They opened the Bibles to Judges and started reading.

Judith gasped a few times. Samson's brutality could be jarring. When kids were taught lessons in Sunday school the stories were usually sugar-coated. Kids probably didn't read the entire text of popular Sunday school lessons until they became adults. A short time later the kids stopped reading and were silent.

Buddy leaned toward him. "That was...weird and phenomenal at the same time."

"Why?" He wanted him to think about what he'd read and express himself clearly.

Before Buddy could reply, Judith leaned toward him. "Well, he was mean. He burned foxes, slaughtered people, that whole thing about the riddle...but even though he was mean God was still behind him."

"Aye. You must remember that this is the Old Testament before Jesus came so there were certain rules about sinning that were not yet put into place."

"Even though it was brutal it was pretty cool too." Buddy seemed to really be getting into it as he glanced at the scripture. "The way he killed that lion with his bare hands? Amazing. He had such great strength. It was almost like he wasn't human. He reminded me of the superheroes."

"Aye. That's why I wanted you two to read that."

"I still can't believe that Delilah tricked him." Buddy seemed confused by this.

Judith sighed. "Buddy, it's obvious how she was able to do that. Men can be so stupid sometimes."

Buddy playfully slapped his sister's shoulder. "Hey, that's not true."

They asked more questions as they continued to discuss Samson. It was such a relief that he'd gotten their minds off the video games for a little while.

Raquel opened her eyes. She'd dozed for a bit after Patrick had gone upstairs. She heard murmuring. Sounded like Patrick was talking to the twins. Such a beautiful thing how he connected with young people. Emily approached Raquel toting the big plastic bag that she'd been carrying earlier. Ah, the Christmas present. She'd forgotten all about that. Well, she needed some cheering up so maybe Emily's gift would take her mind off her worries.

After she'd taken one of the lavender pills and washed it down with some water, Emily gave her the bag. "I bought this as a Christmas gift for one of my friends at church." She shrugged. "But, I think it's something you can use. Might make you feel better."

Raquel peeked into the bag. She pulled out a pink spiral journal and a pink pen with a fake diamond stud at the top. The last thing she removed from the bag was a book of women's devotions. Both of the books had a pretty rose pattern. When she ran her fingers over the journal, the cover felt nice, had a good-feeling texture to it. "Emily, this is so pretty." She hesitated. "I don't want to accept this if it's for somebody else."

"Raquel, just accept the gift. I can always buy another one for my friend."

Surely, the Lord would want her to accept this gift. She fingered the journal. "Thank you, Emily."

"You're welcome." Emily sighed. She then took the nearby thermos and poured some hot coffee into a cup. She took a sip. "I realize you've gone through a lot recently. I can't imagine what it must feel like being told your whole life that your dad was dead, and then you discover that he's alive." She took a deep breath and focused on Raquel. "I wanted to explain why I felt that I needed to give you the journal. I went through a rough time when my dad died."

Raquel nodded as she focused on her cousin's wife. Frank had been hired as an accountant to give financial advice about Emily's family farm. Frank had been hired by Emily's dad before he'd died. Emily's dad had not told Emily about hiring Frank, so when Frank showed up on that first day, Emily had been floored. She wasn't used to letting others advise about the family business. Upon further thought, she realized that Emily was a lot like herself - stubborn, headstrong, and independent. Such traits were admirable, but, sometimes, such traits could prove to be stumbling blocks. "I know that you didn't want Frank advising you about your farm." While Frank had been working on Emily's farm, he'd called Raquel a few times, complaining about his headstrong client.

"I was upset about my dad's sudden death." She paused and took another sip of coffee. Looked like she was gathering her thoughts – trying to be sure she said the right thing. "I was also struggling with my feelings for Frank. As I spent more time with him, I found myself liking him. But, there wasn't anything I could do about my feelings for him. At the time, he wasn't saved and he was an alcoholic. In spite of this, he wouldn't leave my mind. I kept thinking about him and I was also struggling with my grief."

She sighed. "Anyway, it was a rough time for me. Frank and I had feelings for each other, but he admitted that he needed help for his drinking problem. He went back to Chicago. Things got even worse when my stepmom left the farm." Emily's mom had died when she was a kid, and her dad had remarried. Her stepmom had left the farm and relocated so that she could live closer to her biological children – they needed her help – and she'd been anxious to mend the fractured relationship she had with her biological offspring. "I was out here on the farm living by myself for the first time in my life. So, around that time, that's when I started journaling. It helped me to write down my thoughts, struggles, and even my prayers to God. Journaling was a powerful outlet for me." She shrugged. "It might work for you as well. I feel that your situation is drastic and doing what I did might help. You're struggling because of this new information that you found out about your dad. You're also struggling with your feelings for Patrick. Write your feelings down and pray about them. Try not to get so upset that you don't sleep – that causes undue stress for you and for Patrick. I can tell that he still cares for you."

"The thought scares the daylights out of me."

Emily tilted her head. "Why?"

"Because of our fractured past. He left me for a good reason, but, in spite of that, he still left. I don't know if it's a good idea for us to be together again."

Emily patted her shoulder. "I understand. Just think and pray about it. Maybe the two of you can take things slow and just be friends for a while then see what happens after that."

The lights flickered for a few seconds before they came on.

"Mom, the lights are on." The kids rushed down the stairs. They immediately turned on the TV so that they could play their video games.

Raquel's heart thudded with joy. She'd never been so happy to see the return of electricity in her entire life.

Chapter 7

Patrick glanced over at Raquel as they sped down the highway. Twenty-four hours ago, the lights had come on at her cousin Frank's house. Since then, Raquel had spoken to Ama and had confirmed that her father was still alive and that he still was anxious to speak with her in person. Raquel still seemed stressed and tense. Poor lass. He wished there was more that he could do to help her. They'd stopped for a meal a few times. Raquel had claimed she wasn't hungry, but he'd made her eat something.

She continued to scribble in the notebook that Emily had given to her as a Christmas gift. That little book, as well as the book of devotionals, were the two things that seemed to calm her down. As they whizzed past the snow-covered pine trees he stole another look at the notebook. Raquel's face was tense as she wrote. It seemed as if the words she was printing on the page were her link to a better place.

He needed to know what she was writing about. Maybe knowing what was in her mind would help him to understand how to make her feel better. Maybe there was something that he could say or do to make her not quite as tense. He cleared his throat. "Raquel—"

A deer sped from the snow-covered trees. Looked like it was headed straight for the highway.

"Patrick. Watch out." Her voice shrouded with fear as he braced himself for the sudden impact. Miraculously, they were able to keep driving. Raquel glanced behind them. "Looks like the deer stopped and didn't cross the highway."

"Aye, that's a blessing for sure. The horns on those bucks can really mess up your engine."

He glanced at Raquel. She still looked sad as she gazed out the window. She'd put her journal aside. Good. Maybe now was a good time to pick her brain and find out what she'd been writing about. He gestured toward the spiral pink notebook. "What've you been writing about?"

"So much stuff." She sighed and balled her hand into a fist. "My hand is sore from writing so much."

"Take a break. Talk to me. I want to know what's going on with you."

"I can't really tell you...so much is going on in my head right now."

"Well, just talk to me. Try and tell me. I don't want you to get so upset that you faint again." She didn't say anything. Hopefully, she would feel comfortable enough to confide in him. He eyed the dashboard. Their gas tank was almost empty. He suddenly felt tired. Maybe he needed to take a nap. "We need to stop for gas."

He took the exit off the freeway and pulled into a gas station. *Lord if it is Your will, please allow Raquel to confide in me and tell me how she's feeling. Amen.*

Raquel glanced at Patrick. Dark circles shadowed his vivid green eyes. His mouth was mashed down. He was still upset about her fainting. Plus, he was tired. Patrick was always so strong and determined, wanting to do the right thing. Being with someone who cared so deeply for her was touching. She'd been dozing a lot since they left Frank's house. She'd also been writing in her journal. How she wished she could get over her fear of driving so that she could take the wheel for a while. She took a few deep breaths.

They were hours away from the Royal Spring Hospice Center. He needed to sleep for the rest of the trip.

She recalled how Patrick used to worry about her. She needed to be sure that he knew that she was okay. Her mouth watered. Yeah, she was hungry. If she ate something and told Patrick about what was on her mind, then he'd probably feel better. The gas station doubled as a small convenience store. "I'm going to use the bathroom. I'll be back in a few minutes." She rushed into the store. After using the ladies' room, she scanned the store and found some pre-made sandwiches in the refrigerated section. She quickly purchased four chicken salad sandwiches, chips, apples, and water. When she returned to the car, Patrick stoically sat at the wheel, as if eager to get on the road. He clutched a bottle of iced coffee. Good thing he'd not yet opened it. The last thing she needed was for him to stay awake now since he was so exhausted. Yeah, she wanted to see her dad, but, what if Patrick had an accident? No way could she ever forgive herself if that happened.

She gently took his hand. His eyes widened when she pried his pale fingers away from the bottle. She put the bottle aside. "Please stop worrying about me, Patrick." Still holding his hand, she bowed her head. "Lord, thank you for this food, and thank you for allowing me to spend time with Patrick again. Please help us to rest and find comfort while we finish the last leg of our journey. Oh, and Lord, thank you so much for the gift that Emily gave to me. Journaling has helped me to feel a little bit better." She sighed and took a deep breath. "Lord, please be with my dad, help him to heal and get better. Allow him to speak to me before he..." she took another deep breath. "Lord, just allow me to spend some time with my father. Amen." She squeezed Patrick's hand.

"Amen." Patrick's deep voice resonated in the car.

She sighed and glanced toward the highway. "Patrick there's a back-up on the freeway." She turned the radio on.

"There's been a four-car accident on the main freeway. All lanes have been shut down. Helicopters and emergency vehicles have been dispatched." The radio announcer went on to state that the backup could last for hours. She cringed. *Lord, please help those people. Please let your Holy Spirit be with those people involved in the accident. Please comfort and heal them – let them live Lord, with no casualties. Amen.*

Now what could they do? She pressed her hands together. Hopefully, she'd still be able to see her father. She sighed.

"What's the matter Rocky?" He reached over and stroked her back. He used to do that whenever she was anxious, trying to get her to calm down. The tender gesture unlocked her mind with memories of the wonderful times that they used to spend together. Oh, how she'd missed him when he'd left to return to Ireland. He then leaned over and kissed her cheek. His jade green eyes laced with tenderness as he looked at her. Heat swirled through her veins like liquid fire. She glanced at the snowbank in the distance. Maybe if she took a tumble in that thick cold blanket of snow, she'd quench the liquid fire burning through her veins.

His stomach rumbled interrupting the heated moment.

"I think we should eat something." She chuckled. "Sounds like you're hungry."

"Aye. I am. After we eat, you can tell me what's ailing you."

She unwrapped the sandwiches and took a bite. The sweet, slightly tangy taste of the chicken salad exploded into her mouth like a silken delicacy. She gobbled down the sandwich before enjoying the salty crunchy potato chips. She then guzzled the cold bottle of water. Some of the water dripped down her chin. She swiped the moisture away with her hand. "That chicken salad is amazing."

"Aye, it's pretty good." After they'd eaten the sandwiches and chips, she bit into one of the crisp red apples. The sweetness of the apple was a perfect end to their simple meal. After she'd thrown their trash away, he reclined his seat as far as it would go.

Although she was bundled up, the frigid temperatures made her fingers feel like icicles. She removed her gloves from her pocket and slid them on her hands. "You're cold, Rocky. You should've said something." He started the engine and turned the heat on. The gentle purr of the engine proved soothing. Soon heat enveloped the car with warmth.

"Oh, that feels so good. I just didn't think it was a good idea to keep the engine running the entire time while we're stuck."

He shrugged as he leaned back into his reclined seat and closed his eyes. "We'll be fine. What were you worrying about earlier?"

"My dad. I feel like such a failure."

His eyes popped open. "Why?" He looked at her as if he thought she was being ridiculous.

"You looked so tired, and I thought we'd lose time because you needed to rest. I felt that I should drive."

"Don't worry about that. I know you feel bad about your fear of driving. You ever talk to anybody about it? Get some help?"

She shook her head. "No. I've gotten used to taking Uber and my house is only a few blocks away from my coffee shop." She took a few deep breaths. "I guess I've just gotten used to living this way."

When she'd gotten her learner's permit as a teenager her mom had taken her out to practice driving. Right away, she'd had a terrible accident. Her mother had been unharmed, but she'd been in the hospital for two days and it had taken weeks for her broken leg and her broken arm to heal up. Although she'd not been at fault for the accident she'd still been scared. Whenever she got behind the wheel of a car she froze up since the first thing she'd think about was that terrible accident. As a result, she'd never gotten her driver's license.

"Ah, Rocky. It's bothering you right now. You can make a New Year's resolution to learn to drive. I'd be happy to teach you."

She glanced at him. After all this time apart, she'd thought she'd gotten him out of her system – but she hadn't. His piercing green eyes, vivid red hair, pale skin and...muscles. She smiled recalling how they'd sometimes work out at the gym together. She'd get heated as she'd looked at him. Again, she recalled the passionate nights they'd shared. Blowing air through her lips, she peeked at him again. His teaching her to drive was not a good idea. Not. At. All.

Since he'd returned to town and was helping her, that didn't mean that they'd pick up where they left off...did it?

He closed his eyes again. Probably wanted to get a few hours of sleep before the traffic cleared up. During their trip, she'd been scribbling in her journal. She'd been writing down every single thing that she could recall her mom telling her about her "dead" father. People were always telling her that she had a sharp memory. So if something was really important to her, she seldom forgot about it.

Not only had she written about her dad.

She'd also written about Patrick.

It bothered her that he'd never asked her to come to Ireland with him. He never even invited her to come visit. She supposed the breakup was cleaner that way, with minimal contact between them.

But, after all this time, he still haunted her mind – and that made her feel weak and somewhat insecure. She considered herself a strong woman – but – being around Patrick...well, she needed to pray about this, long and hard. She swallowed as a troublesome thought lurked in her mind. During their road trip she'd found out that Patrick was acquainted with a few people who worshipped at her church. She figured that's where he would worship. What if he started dating one of the church members? How could she take seeing him dating another woman, cozying up with someone – when she still thought about him?

Oh Lord, what am I supposed to do? She balled her hands into fists and silently prayed to Jesus. She wanted to know the truth. She looked at him again. He was laying there right beside her. She had a question that was burning in her mind like an overdone biscuit. He was still awake. She could tell because he wasn't snoring.

"Patrick." He immediately opened his eyes at the abrupt tone of her voice.

"What is it lass?"

Ask him to tell you the truth. The words settled into her gut like a warm, soothing ocean. Almost felt as if God were placing those words into her mind to make her feel better. She licked her lips and took several deep breaths. She could do this. She had to. "When you left to go to back to Ireland to live and to take care of your sisters..."

Nervousness enveloped her as she pressed her hands together. Patrick reached over and placed his hand over hers. The gentle warmth from his touch soothed her. "Go on." His deep voice, soft and encouraging, was just what she needed to hear.

"Why didn't you ask me to come with you?" There. She'd said it.

Patrick removed his hand from hers. His mouth pressed into a thin line. He raised his seat back up. Uh oh. Looked like he wasn't going to be able to take his nap after all. "We don't have to talk about this now."

He was hiding something. She could feel it. Perhaps he'd quickly found a new girlfriend in Ireland and he didn't want to hurt her feelings. But, if he had a girlfriend in Ireland, why'd he relocate back here? Sure, he wanted a relationship with his dad, but...did he want to reunite with *her* as well?

He opened the door and cold wind exploded into the vehicle. Shivering she glared at him. "Where are you going?"

"I need to take a walk. I'll be back in a few." He slammed the door and stormed away, obviously angry.

Now, what was that all about?

Chapter 8

The cold wind sliced through his thick jacket like a knife. His frigid lips trembled as he scampered down the snowy path. Too bad he'd forgotten his gloves in the car. Well, he needed some time away from Raquel. No way could he tell her *why* he'd never asked her to join him when he'd returned to Ireland. Sure, he'd missed her every single day. But, if he'd asked her to come, she would have given up so much. She'd probably would've resented him, and he just couldn't imagine being weighed down with the guilt...but that wasn't the only reason he'd not asked her to come with him.

His mum and *why* she'd died. *How* she'd died. Frigid cold enveloped him – reminded him of how it might feel to be trapped inside an ice cube. He glanced at the highway. Traffic was still backed up. He shoved his hands into the pockets of his coat. After he'd walked for fifteen minutes dots of wetness landed on his face. Snow. Thick gentle flakes descended from the heavens. Hopefully there wouldn't be any more accumulation. They certainly didn't need anything else to hold them up from seeing Rocky's dad before he died.

He glanced at his SUV. Snow obscured the windshield so he couldn't see Rocky's face. Maybe the Lord was trying to tell him something. Maybe He didn't want him and Rocky to make the trip right now. Maybe being delayed would force him to be honest with her about what really happened to his mum. If he really wanted to make a fresh start with Raquel, she had to know everything. If he kept secrets from her, well, then there'd be no way that their relationship could work. With measured steps he approached his vehicle. His hands were so stiff with cold that he could barely open the door.

The door popped open. Rocky leaned toward him after she'd opened the door for him. He guessed she'd seen him struggling. Her dark brown eyes looked troubled. Well, they needed to have a good long talk.

As Patrick got into the vehicle, she studied his face. Tense. Upset. He placed his reddened, obviously ice-cold hands, against the heat ducts. "It's nippy out there."

"Are you mad at me?"

He stopped rubbing his hands and looked directly at her. "No. I'm angry. Not at you. I'm angry at myself."

This was surprising. "What do you mean?"

He took her hand. His pale skin was still drenched with cold. She covered his hand with both of hers. "Rocky, there's stuff about my mum, that I didn't tell you." He didn't say anything for a few seconds. "I'll tell you about that later."

She nodded. "Okay." She just wanted him to tell her what was on his mind. Hopefully he wouldn't take too long.

"Well, one reason why I didn't ask you to come with me...well...you were determined to open your coffee shop. You'd started scouting for possible locations. Making a business plan. I couldn't ask you to give that up to come with me. You'd start resenting me. I know it."

She gulped. Yeah, she'd have been disappointed. Butterscotch Bliss had been a dream come true. She loved her little shop. She was passionate about making pastries that people enjoyed. Whenever she spotted a new customer tasting her buns for the first time – and seeing that delighted expression after that first bite...well, that made her day. She remained silent, digesting what he'd just revealed. "You didn't give me a chance to even make the decision. I might have been able to open a coffee shop in Ireland. Have you ever thought about that?"

"Aye, I did. But, I didn't think it would be the same for you."

"That's the *only* reason you didn't ask me to come?"

"No." His lips mashed down as he stared at their joined hands. "My mum. I feel uncomfortable telling you why she died."

"She had a sudden heart attack. You already told me about that." Since he'd been gone for a few years perhaps he'd forgotten that he'd already shared this information with her.

"Yeah, she had a heart attack, but, I didn't tell you why she had one." He took a deep breath. "My mum...Rocky...she was sick. Not well."

She narrowed her eyes and looked directly at his face. "What do you mean?" She tried to keep her voice soft and gentle. She didn't want him to know that it angered her that he'd keep secrets from her, especially after all the time they'd spent together.

"She was depressed. Her problem was mental. She...she killed herself Rocky. Took her own life."

Her lips quivered. The impact of what he'd just revealed slammed into her - jolting her out of her comfort zone.

Tears splattered his pale cheeks.

She'd never seen Patrick cry.

She gulped. *Lord, please help me to say the right words.* "Patrick, I'm so sorry." She tried to hug him but he pulled away. He shook his head as he folded his arms in front of him, almost as if he were creating an invisible shield between them. "My sisters. They found her. She died of a heart attack caused by the overdose."

Lord have mercy. Those poor children. Speechless, she sensed she needed to give Patrick time to finish what he had to say before she interrupted. She didn't attempt to hug him again, but she did pray. *Jesus. Jesus. Jesus.* Shocked, all she could do was say Jesus's name over and over during the moment of silence.

"The twins, me...only some close family members know what happened. We just revealed that she'd died of a heart attack. We...we didn't want people to know everything."

She nodded. She could understand why he didn't want to publicly reveal every detail about her death. She wondered how the twins were coping. She was about to ask, but then recalled that she wanted to give him time to tell her everything that he needed to say. "One of the twins has depression. I worry. I know I need to leave everything in God's hands but, I still worry about her. That's why I call them so often." He took a deep breath. "Rocky, I was in love with you. I still love you."

Her heart skipped a beat. She then jerked back, shocked that he'd state this right now. "I came back to apologize to you about how I broke up with you. I feel bad about what happened. I just couldn't dump that entire situation on you. I was a mess." He looked directly at her. "You couldn't be with me back then. I was a drunken mess."

So many tumultuous feelings thundered through her. How could she process all of this right now? Patrick had told her when they'd first started dating that he didn't drink. He'd been sober for a few years and was proud of it. However, it appeared that his mom's death shattered his sobriety.

"Our aunt and uncle lived with us for a few months after mum died. Helped me to cope with my problems and helped out with the twins. I found a job and knew that the Lord wanted me to be there for my sisters. I had to be strong for them. At first I was a weak mess, but, now...well, I think my faith is stronger. I insisted that the girls go to church with me each Sunday. I want them to lean on Jesus. I know how things can get murky and it's hard, but..." he shrugged as if he were unsure how to finish his statement.

Whoa, now what was she going to do. She didn't think that she could just welcome Patrick back into her life with open arms. Did he have other secrets?

He said that he loved her – but so much time had passed. Did he simply love the memories of the time they'd spent together, or, did he really *love* her for the woman that she was right now?

"You're upset." He peeked over at her and tried to grab her hand. She pulled away.

"Give me a minute." She closed her eyes. *Lord, help me to say the right thing.* "I'm sorry about your mom. I feel bad for the twins. Do you think they'll be okay?" When her mom had passed, she'd been devastated. She could imagine it being worse if one were a teenager. Knowing that their mom took her own life – how would a youngster cope with something so awful?

"Both have been in therapy for a long time. They know that they must let me know if they need any help." He took a deep breath. "They're doing fine – adjusting to life without their mum. Seemed weird sending them off to college without mum around."

He jerked his thumb toward the highway. "Traffic is picking up. Maybe we can get on the road to try and see your dad."

She nodded. After he'd started up the engine he drove down the packed snowy path and onto the highway. She glanced at the evergreens weighed down with so much snow that their branches swung toward the ground. White-capped mountains rose toward the heavens in the distance. Such a beautiful day. She glanced at her journal and pen resting in the back seat. She just couldn't journal right now.

Patrick remained quiet. She wasn't sure if he was mad at himself for telling her the truth about his mom, or, if he was being considerate – giving her time to digest what he'd just revealed. The information was a lot to take in so suddenly. Yeah, they'd talk about it more later. But, right now, she needed to see her dad. She eyed the clock. Only a few more hours before they reached their destination.

Patrick pulled into a parking space at the Royal Spring Hospice Center. Snow clung to the bare branches of a nearby tree. He focused on the frosty moisture of the branches, taking deep breaths. He yawned. Boy he could really go for a good night's rest. "We're here, Rocky." He reached over and gently shook her. She'd been sleeping for the past hour. He'd been silent for the rest of their journey, wanting to give her time to come to terms with what he'd revealed about his mum. He also wanted to give her some space. He knew she was anxious about seeing her dad.

"Patrick. I'm so scared."
"Remember what you said about trusting in Jesus."

Yeah, she trusted in Jesus, but she was still scared. *Lord, help me.*

"Maybe you should call Ama. Let her know we're here."

Now, that was a good idea. Ama had given her the room number and told her that she needed to sign in at the front desk. She quickly pulled out her phone and called Ama. After a few rings, it went straight to voicemail. "I guess she can't answer right now."

"She might be sleeping. Must be tough, sitting with your husband while he's dying."

Raquel blinked and took a deep breath. Her heart skipped. She grabbed Patrick's hand.

"Babe, what's wrong?"

"What you just said about Ama...Patrick, I've been so selfish. Self absorbed."

"What do you mean?"

"Well, I've been so upset about my mom not telling me about my dad being alive, that I never considered what Ama has been going through. Since I've found out about my dad, I've been absorbed with self-pity, upset about not knowing he's been alive all these years. Not once have I thought about or prayed for Ama."

"Ah, Rocky. Stop worrying. I'm sure Ama understands that you have a lot on your mind. Finding out that the father whom you thought has been dead for your entire life, is really alive, is a lot to digest. Most would have reacted as you have." He gestured toward the building. "We need to go inside if you're going to speak with your father."

She'd been so anxious to arrive in time and now she was stalling. Yes, they'd better go inside. Before she could open her door Patrick rushed out of the car and quickly opened her door for her. He took her hand and helped her out of the vehicle. "Careful now. Icy out here. Wouldn't want you to slip." His calm caring deep voice comforted her. Just knowing he was beside her helped her to not feel so leery about entering the building. Still holding her hand, he opened the door. A thick alcohol-like scent filled the air. The lobby was quiet. A Christmas tree rested in the corner. Multi-colored lights winked on the tree. Festive wrapped gifts surrounded it.

"May I help you?" A middle-aged male desk clerk smiled at them. They approached the desk.

"I'm here to see Gregory Montague. Room 126."

The clerk nodded. After checking their IDs he pointed to the clipboard. "Just sign in and go on back."

She grabbed the pen and hesitated. For some reason the urge to tell the clerk that Greg was her dad wrestled within her. But, she just couldn't mouth those words to a stranger – at least not yet. What would she say when she saw him? What would she call him? Would she call him dad? Uncle Greg? Mr. Montague? Calling him Mr. Montague sounded too formal, stiff, stilted.

Patrick touched her hand. "You okay, Rocky?" His deep voice was gentle. His tone concerned. The last thing she needed was for him to start worrying about her again. She bit her lower lip, still clutching the pen. Well, she'd tell him what she'd been thinking later. She needed to put his mind at ease so that he wouldn't be upset. "I'm just nervous is all."

He narrowed his eyes. He didn't believe her. He knew she was upset, but she figured he wouldn't press for details right now. After all, they'd made a long journey and now it was time for her to see her dad for the first time in her life – well, for the first time that she could remember. She quickly scrawled her name on the clipboard and Patrick did the same. When they approached room 126 the door was ajar. The medicinal odor was stronger as the door opened.

The bed was empty. A young worker stood at the foot of the bed folding a blanket. She glanced up at them. "Good evening. May I help you?"

Raquel gulped. Before she could respond Patrick came to her rescue. "We're here to see Gregory Montague."

"Oh, I'm afraid you're too late. He's gone."

She squeezed her eyes shut and clutched the doorknob. Gone? Her father had died after all! Her heart thundered with dread as Patrick pulled her into his arms.

Chapter 9

Patrick focused on the worker who'd just spoken. No way would an employee deliver such devastating news so casually. He needed some answers. "Too late? Are you saying that Gregory Montague has passed away?" He simply couldn't bring himself to say the word 'died'.

The young woman's eyes rounded. The blanket fell from her hands as she focused on them. "Oh, my goodness. My bad." She came closer. "Gregory Montague is not dead. Please don't tell my boss about what I just said. They said I needed to improve my bedside manner, so, that's what I'm trying to do."

Relief flowed through his veins like golden honey. He let out the breath that he didn't even realize he'd been holding. Raquel relaxed too, but still snuggled against him. "Well, where is he?" Her pretty voice sounded small and scared. She was obviously still apprehensive about seeing her dad and wanted to get the initial meeting over with.

"There were some complications."

"Complications?" Concern etched Raquel's voice as she awaited the worker's next words.

"Yes. You'll need to go to Royal Spring Community Hospital down the street. Check in at the front desk. The doctor should be able to provide more information."

"Thanks." He grabbed Raquel's hand and together they quickly walked to the car. He revved the engine and with the help of the GPS they arrived at the hospital in minutes.

They quickly walked toward the building. Raquel's foot hit an icy patch and she slammed down onto the sidewalk. Darts of pain shot through her knee as Patrick gently helped her up. "Rocky, I'm so sorry."

"Don't apologize. It's not your fault that I fell." She winced as they made their way into the hospital. Her knee was so sore that she had to limp.

After giving their information to the woman at the front desk, the woman sadly shook her head. "We can't allow visitors right now. Only immediate family members."

Raquel stood up as straight as her sore knee would allow. "I'm his daughter." She leaned toward the desk clerk. "I need to see him." The woman appeared taken aback, before she gave Raquel a name tag. Raquel scrawled her name on the tag, her hand shaking. She then removed the sticky piece of paper and pressed it onto her shirt.

The worker eyed Patrick. "He can't go in there with you. Against the rules."

"I'll wait here for you." He gestured toward the couch in the corner. "I'll be sitting right there praying for you the entire time."

When Patrick made a promise he meant it. That was one of the things she loved about him. He caressed her face with his big gentle hands. Shivers of hot warmth flowed through her. She shook her head, clearing thoughts of Patrick. She needed to focus on her father. Not saying another word, she limped toward the elevator and took it up to the fifth floor – which was the floor where her father was resting right now.

Patrick slumped onto the couch. *Jesus help Raquel---*

His phone vibrated. Oh no, it was his dad. "Hi Dad."

"Patrick have you started the profitability review yet? I'm still waiting for it."

"No." He quickly gave his father a rundown about all that had occurred since they'd started their trip. "So, she just went back to see her father. I'm so tired that I can barely keep my eyes open. Did you reschedule the meeting?"

"Yes, it's tomorrow."

Tomorrow? No way could he have the report done by then. If he had a strong pot of coffee he might be able to sit up all night in order to give his father a draft. "I'll have it to you day after tomorrow. I promise."

"I'll have my secretary to move the meeting." From the abrupt tone of his voice he sounded as if he was unhappy about the change. He paused. Sounded like he wanted to say something else.

"Was there anything else?" He mentally sighed. Hopefully his dad wasn't too upset.

"Just keep me posted about Raquel."

"Okay." He rang off with his father. Well, at least he seemed concerned about Raquel so that was good. He still wanted to make a good impression on his dad and have a positive working relationship. Hopefully the relationship could bleed into their personal relationship. However, fatigue swept through his body. He removed his shoes and laid on the couch. His energy should be restored by tomorrow.

He'd work on his presentation and possibly impress his dad. *Jesus, please help Raquel...* He closed his eyes.

Raquel limped down the hallway as fast as she could. *Lord help me. Lord help me. Lord help me.* She mentally chanted those words as she opened the door to her father's room. An elderly man rested beneath a blanket. The man's dark skin contrasted with the snowy white sheets. His eyes were closed. He had a deep even breathing pattern. Tubes ran out of his nose. She spotted an oxygen tank close by. His hair reminded her of thick gray wool. Slowly, as if sensing her presence, he opened his eyes and peered directly at her. "You came." His words sounded raspy – almost as if his throat were dry and he needed a drink of water.

"Did you need some water?" She managed to say the words but didn't realize she cried until her hot wet tears splattered onto the blanket.

He barely nodded. After a bit of fiddling around with the controls on the bed, she managed to raise the bed a bit. She then poured a small cup of water from the pitcher beside the bed. She held the cup to his lips. He took a long drink. He then rested back onto the pillow. It was almost as if drinking the water drained all of the energy from his body. "Thank you." The words were barely a whisper.

She had so many questions – questions that she didn't know if she should ask right now. She glanced around the room and found a folding chair in the corner. She pulled the chair close to his bed and sat down. Then taking his brown wrinkled hand, she held it, squeezed his wrinkled fingers. "Is it okay if I call you Greg?" Saying 'dad' just sounded too familiar, too formal. She wanted to talk to him. No, she *needed* to talk to him. She wanted to make sure that both of them were comfortable with the conversation that was about to take place.

He nodded.

Well, as awkward as this was, she needed to get the ball rolling. Her father didn't look well, not at all. And she'd come as he'd requested. If he had the energy and was willing to talk, then she would just ask about what was on her mind. "Why did my mom tell me that you were dead? Why didn't you ever come to visit me?" Well, that was two questions, hopefully, he would be able to respond.

"I was no good. Had a drug problem. Couldn't keep a job." His eyes teared. He squeezed her hand. "I was bad to your mom. You were a baby…" More tears slid down his cheeks. "I attacked your mom. I was high on drugs. I knew she had some money, and she wouldn't give it to me." Startled, she dropped his hand. His nose started running so she grabbed a Kleenex and wiped the mucous away. Her heart thundered in her chest. "Beat her up so bad, she was in the hospital for a few days. She got a restraining order against me." He sniffed and kept looking at her with his watery brown eyes – eyes that reminded her of her own. "Your mom wanted to protect you – protect you from me. I don't blame her. She only wanted…wanted to do what was best for you."

Whoa, what in the world was she going to do? Just hearing these things made her feel awful. Her mom had been the gentlest, sweetest, kindest person she'd ever known, and to think that this man attacked her for no good reason? She took another Kleenex and balled it into her fist. She thought about his words for a few minutes while she squeezed the tissue. "What happened after you beat up my mom?"

"I was homeless. Living on the streets for five years. Did some crime. Went into prison for ten."

Her eyes widened. "Ten years?"

He slowly nodded. "Prison was the best thing that happened to me." She peered at him. Surely he was talking crazy. How could being in prison be good? She pushed the negative thought away as she recalled that the Apostle Paul had been imprisoned for preaching the Gospel. "Oh, baby girl, prison's a rough place. Rough. But, while there, I couldn't get drugs. I had time to think about all the mistakes that I'd made." He coughed. She gave him another drink of water. He then continued. "I got saved while in prison. Christians came every week to talk to us and we had church. I wrote your mama a letter, telling her how sorry I was and that I'd been saved." He paused for a few seconds. "She never wrote me back. I don't blame her. I was a mean person. I didn't treat her with respect."

She jerked, recalling the ugly jagged scar on her mom's arm. She'd asked her mom about it a few times, and all she'd said was that she'd been in a terrible fight when she was younger. It never made any sense since her mom didn't seem to be one who'd been prone to getting into fights. "Did you...did you cut my mom's arm?"

He briefly closed his eyes. "Yes. As I said, I was high. I had a sharp piece of glass. I cut her arm. She screamed. You woke up and started crying." He coughed again. "Your cries broke into my trance. For some reason I got scared and I left."

She didn't know if she wanted to get to know him better after she heard how mean he was to her mom. Anger, as hot as a boiling stew, simmered within her – she imagined the simmering anger could erupt into lava - like a volcano. She'd talked to people at church who'd told her how hard it was to let go of anger. *Forgive him.* The words, as clean and fresh as newly fallen snow, popped into her mind.

"Please forgive me."

She didn't know if she could forgive him right now. At this very minute. At this moment, forgiveness would have to be a journey. "I...I don't know if I can."

"Just try baby girl."

He kept calling her baby girl. Maybe she should remind him that her name was Raquel. She opened her mouth, then closed it. For some reason, she kind of liked his calling her baby girl. Perhaps her acceptance of the nickname was her first step into forgiving him.

The door opened, interrupting their conversation. "Oh, thank God you were able to come." Ama breezed into the room. Not giving Raquel time to say anything, she hugged her and kissed her on the cheek. "I've been praying for you to come and you have." Raquel hugged the chunky brown-skinned woman. She smelled like soap and hairspray.

Thoughts of what her dad had just confessed, her long trip to see her dad, and the information that Patrick had shared about his mom tumbled through her mind like a vicious cyclone. Unable to control herself, she whimpered, a loud sound erupted from the room. It took a moment for Raquel to realize it was the sound of her own voice, crying. Uncontrollable tears leaked from her eyes as Ama continued to embrace her, rubbing her back, cooing as if she were trying to console an injured child.

Chapter 10

Patrick yawned as he emailed the profitability review to his father. He wanted to see if his dad had any questions. The meeting was scheduled for the following day. He eyed the time on his laptop. Eight o'clock PM. Ama was at the hospital. Raquel was in the spare bedroom. They'd bunked at Ama's the previous evening. Raquel had refused to go to the hospital with Ama today. He knew it would take time for her to forgive her dad. But she had a kind heart so in due time he felt that she would do as the Lord wanted her to.

He stood up and stretched. Since Raquel's dad continued to stay in the hospital, one of the members at Ama's church had brought over a casserole for their dinner. He scooped some onto a paper plate and warmed it into the microwave. The delicious smell of melted cheese, meat and potatoes filled the kitchen. His stomach grumbled. When the microwave dinged he removed the hot plate of food. He found cutlery in a nearby drawer. A large pitcher of iced tea rested on the top shelf of the refrigerator. He dropped ice cubes into a glass and poured a cup of tea.

He sat at the table. *Lord, thank you for this food. Please be with Raquel, Greg, and Ama. Please Lord, if it's Your will, could you heal Greg? Raquel needs to see her father in a positive light. Amen.*

He shoved a bite of food into his mouth. The cheesy goodness filled his mouth with happiness. In spite of all the negative things going on in his and Raquel's lives, he smiled. Food sometimes had a way of making one feel better. He finished his food in minutes and washed it down with the iced tea. As he leaned back and relaxed in the kitchen chair he closed his eyes and thought about all that he'd learned over the last day.

Ama had mentioned that Greg had cancer. He'd gotten worse so they'd transported him to the hospital. What had been strange was when Ama had come home earlier to shower she'd said that his condition had stabilized a little bit. She mentioned that the doctor said that sometimes that happened not long before a patient died.

Raquel had not said much. She'd spent a lot of time talking on the phone to Emily and Frank. She'd also been scribbling in her journal. He made sure that she knew that she could approach him if she needed him for anything. He was able to focus on work while Raquel stayed busy with her journal writing.

He planned on speaking with her tomorrow morning as soon as she got up. He was going to try to convince her to visit her dad in the hospital, even if it was only for a few minutes.

Patrick hummed as the song *Amazing Grace* filled the sanctuary. The choir, dressed in red robes stood in the pulpit, swaying, their voices lifted in song. Patrick scanned the sea of brown-skinned people standing in the pews – swaying to the music. He closed his eyes and swayed back and forth. A memory, as vivid and fresh as newly fallen snow snapped into his mind. He remembered when he was about five or six he, his mum and his dad had attended church together. The choir had sung *Amazing Grace*. His mum had been so moved by the song. She'd openly cried when the lyrics were sung. His dad had hugged her while she cried. Afterwards they'd gone home for lunch. Was his mum really moved by the music, or, had that been a sign that she'd been deeply depressed? He took a deep breath and opened his eyes.

He was the only white person attending this impromptu service for Raquel's dad at the First Baptist Church of Royal Spring. It felt different...strange, being the only white person amidst a sea of African-Americans. He and Raquel had attended church together twice back when they were dating years ago. The church had been a multicultural church. Greg and Ama attended an all-black church. The only reason that Raquel and Ama were not present during this service is because they remained at the hospital with Raquel's dad. They were looking at the service virtually. He'd been glad that Raquel had finally visited her dad in the hospital.

He again closed his eyes and thought about all that had occurred over the past week. For the first time in years, he'd fasted. For two days, while Raquel struggled with her anger against her dad, Patrick had prayed for Raquel to forgive her father.

He'd also continued praying for her father's recovery.

When Ama had contacted their pastor, telling that Greg had been hospitalized, her congregation had scheduled an impromptu church service to talk and pray for Greg's healing. When Patrick had first entered the church, he'd been stunned that so many people had arrived. He'd just assumed an impromptu service would not have so much interest.

Several people approached him, introducing themselves. He introduced himself as a friend of Raquel's. He highly doubted she'd want him to introduce himself as her boyfriend.

His musings were interrupted when the music stopped and the pastor approached the pulpit. Tasting salt on his upper lip, he wiped his wet eyes. He'd not realized he'd been crying.

For him, crying meant shame – but right now, well, he needed to do what he could to help Raquel. As the pastor said his prayer, Patrick added his own prayer – prayer for Raquel's forgiveness and for the healing of Gregory Montague.

Raquel approached her father's room in the hospital. She swallowed. It was the day after the impromptu church service. During the service they'd begged God to heal her dad.

Patrick had been a rock of support the entire week. Praying for her and lifting her up. Her anger against her dad had consumed her. Her mom had been the sweetest and kindest person she'd ever known. Just thinking about the abuse she'd endured made her angry. Amidst all of this Patrick had not only supported her but he'd also been talking to his dad on a regular basis. He'd been working remotely and filling his dad in on a special project for his job. Hopefully his dad wouldn't be too upset when they arrived back to the Outer Banks.

She pushed the door open to her father's room. A middle-aged dark-skinned staff member stood at the foot of the bed with a clip board in his hand. "Good morning." She greeted the staff member.

"Oh, hi." The man smiled and introduced himself. "I'm Doctor Brown." There were several doctors who'd been caring for her father. She'd not yet met this one.

"Pleased to meet you."

He pointed to the clipboard. "Puzzling. Your father's vitals have improved overnight. If this keeps up, he might be able to go home."

Shock, as deep and rich as an avalanche cascaded through her veins. She covered her quivering mouth with her hand. "Are you saying he's getting better?"

He nodded. "Looks like it." He shook his head. His brow furrowed. "I don't understand it. As long as I've been practicing medicine, I've never seen anything so baffling and miraculous. I've read of such healings in medical journals but have never experienced it with one of my patients." He continued talking, but, she was too stunned to listen. Her dad slept. His peaceful-sounding snores filled the room. After the doctor exited, she immediately called Ama.

Ama slid the picnic basket into the backseat of Patrick's SUV. "I've packed you some sandwiches for the road. There's also chips, apples and bottles of water." Patrick nodded toward Raquel's stepmother.

"Thanks."

"I know you all have a long trip home. I appreciate you coming. I wanted to do something to thank you."

They'd been staying with Ama for over a week. He eyed Raquel. She hugged her stepmom before getting into the car. She looked...different. He knew she still struggled with forgiving her dad. She'd continued calling Emily for advice. She'd also been calling her assistant Brooke to be sure the coffee house was still running smoothly. Her dad had been at home for one day. A nurse was scheduled daily to care for him as his health continued to improve.

As they pulled out of the driveway they waved to Ama. He scanned the roads as they made their way onto the interstate. A lot of the snow had melted. Some of it still clung to the top of the evergreens that they passed on the highway. He remained silent as they drove. Raquel would speak when she was ready to talk. Her journal rested on the backseat. Her hands pressed together, as if she was anxious about something. Okay, she seemed downright upset so he needed to say something.

"Something bothering you, Rocky?"

"Yeah." The hard edge to her voice, from that one single word, was alarming. He glanced over at her. "I thought my father was going to die but he miraculously healed. I'm still having a hard time accepting how badly he treated my mom."

"His healing was a blessing, Rocky. Forgiveness is a journey. As Christians we must forgive."

"Were you angry at your mom when she did that to herself?" The hard edge to her voice remained. He inwardly winced.

"Aye. I was angry for a long time. My mum was struggling. So was your dad."

A few hours later he pulled into a rest stop. They used the restrooms. Afterwards they opened the picnic basket and feasted on the lunch that Ama had prepared for them. The sandwiches tasted amazing – both spicy and sweet. As he gobbled his lunch, he stole glances at Raquel. She ate half of a sandwich and drank some water. Circles were beneath her eyes. Looked like she'd not gotten enough sleep the night before.

"Maybe you should get some rest. Close your eyes and try to sleep for the rest of the trip."

She shook her head. "I'm too upset and wired to sleep."

He wanted to know if she'd had any time to think about what he'd revealed about his mom, and his reasons for returning to the Outer Banks. Would she be open to spending time with him again? Her mouth tamped down as she peeked at a few squirrels frolicking nearby. Now probably was not a good time to bring up that subject. He figured she wasn't ready to discuss their pursuing a relationship, or even a friendship, right now.

She turned and looked directly at him. The sadness in her dark brown eyes, laced with her fatigue, tugged at him. The urge to hold her consumed him. He reached over and took her hand and squeezed it. "What is it Rocky?" He voiced the question softly, hoping that she'd open up to him. She'd already mentioned what was bothering her – but he sensed that something else was going on.

"What you said…about us spending time together as a couple and me giving you another chance."

"Go on."

He caressed her slim delicate brown fingers as his heart thundered in his chest. *Lord, I want things to work out between us. Please let us be friends, and hopefully, that friendship will grow into something beautiful.*

"I have so much going on right now." She sighed, her shoulders slumping. "I feel sad. I'm struggling with forgiving my dad. I'm also trying to find the courage to bond with him. I believe that's what God wants me to focus on right now."

He winced. If the Lord was calling her to do those things, then he'd have to honor that. No way was he going to stand in her way. She needed time away from him so that she could figure things out. He understood. He just didn't know how to respond. It'd probably be rude for him to remain silent during the rest of the trip. He knew that he had something to say. He just needed to figure out the best way to tell her how he felt. After they'd thrown away the trash from their lunch, he started his vehicle and pulled onto the interstate.

Thankfully Raquel slept most of the way home. He pulled into her driveway at four in the morning. The sky – black as ink – winked with a few silver stars. She slowly opened her eyes. She started to open her door. He reached over and took her hand. "Rocky, I know you're going through a lot and you need to think about...well...everything. Everything that I told you about my mum, and all that's happened with your dad. I'll be praying for you Rocky."

"Thanks." She whispered the word softly, but still didn't look at him.

With his other hand, he gently took her chin between his thumb and index finger and coaxed her to look directly at him. "I know you're hurting right now. You need some time to yourself. Why don't we meet up on Christmas day? That will give you some time to think about the idea of us spending time together." He took a deep breath. "It will also give you time to process forgiving your dad."

She nodded. "Okay."

He released her chin, swallowed, then closed his eyes for a few seconds. "My faith is important to me. So, I'll be going to church, the same one we attended a few times years ago. If I see you at church or around town I promise to just say hello and then just leave you alone. I won't bother you."

She nodded. Then she quickly opened her car door, not giving him a chance to do it for her. She rushed to her house, unlocked the door, and went inside.

Chapter 11

Raquel slammed the dough onto the counter. Her floured hands worked the dough, kneading it with her fingers. Later, she'd be baking a batch of her Butterscotch Bliss buns to serve in her coffee shop. She lifted the dough and slammed it down again. Kneading dough usually calmed her down when she was stressed. The previous night Ama had again called, wanting to know if she could speak with her dad.

She'd still declined. She'd asked Ama about his health and Ama said that he was still getting better and that they were both still praying for her forgiveness.

She'd also been thinking about Patrick. It'd been one week since they'd returned from their trip to see her dad. Every night she'd thought about him. A few times she'd even dreamed about him. The kisses they'd shared. The time they'd spent together years ago was full of love, laughter and joy. Could that joy possibly be recaptured?

Their breakup had been left unfinished, partially unexplained. Now that he'd told her what had happened, she'd been blessed with finally hearing the truth. She wondered if he had other secrets.

Oh, it was times like these when she missed her mom. She longed to have a hot cup of coffee and some of her mom's favorite shortbread cookies. Oh, what a treat that would be if she could just sit and talk with her mom for five minutes. That would make her feel better.

"You're slamming that dough like you got something on your mind." Brooke, her young assistant, breezed into the kitchen. Her white apron stretched across her ample stomach. Brooke did jazzercise regularly since she was determined to lose some weight.

"I'm working off the stress of a sleepless night."

Brooke grunted. "You still stressing over Patrick?" The young woman shook her head. "Sounds like that man's done a lot for you. Did you even thank him for taking you to see your dad on such short notice?"

She stopped mixing the dough. Had she thanked Patrick? She winced, embarrassment spilling into her veins like hot molasses. She honestly couldn't recall if she'd thanked him for his kindness – be a huge shame if she hadn't. How selfish of her. "I don't think so."

Brooke had met Patrick the previous Sunday at church. Raquel had shown her a picture of Patrick so Brooke knew what he looked like. Raquel had been too chicken to attend church. She just wasn't ready to face Patrick yet. So, she'd stayed home and watched the service virtually.

"Raquel, I wanted to tell you something."

She raised her eyebrows. "What?"

"Well, after church, two women approached Patrick." Brooke giggled. Since she was only nineteen years old, Brooke reminded her of a child sometimes.

Okay, it was obvious her assistant wasn't going to tell her until she asked. "What'd these women want?"

She laughed out loud, playfully hitting Raquel's shoulder. "His phone number. Don't take too long to make up your mind. Someone is going to snatch up that man." She took a deep breath. "Girl, he's even better looking in person. He's so tall, those broad shoulders, fiery red hair and deep voice. Plus he's just...well, he seems so nice. I can tell from what you've told me about your road trip that he really likes you. Why don't you give him a chance?" She'd not mentioned to Brooke that she was meeting Patrick on Christmas day to talk about their relationship.

The feeling was mutual, but, she needed to get her life straight before she started dating somebody. She wasn't sure if Brooke could understand that. She didn't respond to Brooke's comments. When Brooke had aged out of the foster care system, her foster parents weren't thrilled about her staying with them since they'd no longer be receiving payment from the government for her upkeep. Raquel had gladly agreed to let her live in the upstairs apartment of her coffee shop, rent free. She'd hired Brooke and taught her how to bake and how to run a business. Brooke was a loner and didn't accept others into her life easily. Raquel supposed Brooke's lack of trust sprouted from being bounced around to different foster homes.

She circumvented her assistant's curiosity the way she usually did – she gave her a task. "Chop up those nuts." Brooke nodded and removed the large cutting board from the shelf. She poured the nuts onto the wood surface and expertly chopped them with a clean knife.

"Hmm...." Brooke seemed to be thinking as she continued chopping nuts. "Well, just remember that it's not as if he broke up with you because he didn't *love* you. Sometimes life gets in the way, right? At least the man loves his family. After his momma died, he moved back to Ireland to care for his teenaged half-sisters. That's devotion. I wished I had someone in my family that cared for me like that instead of abandoning me in foster care." Brooke obviously had a chip on her shoulder from being in the foster care system. She couldn't fault the young woman for her anger – heck, everybody was probably angry about something.

She thought about Brooke's words as they continued preparing the buns. Memories of her relationship with Patrick swirled through her mind like scattered snowflakes. She'd made more buns than usual since they'd sold out the last few days. The delicious smell of spun sugar and dough wrapped the coffee shop like a warm blanket. Brooke brewed large vats of the three types of coffee they'd serve that morning. Raquel flipped the sign on the door from *closed* to *open*. She then rushed back to the counter to begin her workday. Brooke expertly placed the trays of hot buns behind the glass display case.

Late that morning Raquel set out the sandwiches she'd prepared for the lunch crowd. Her mouth watered. She'd been so preoccupied that morning that she'd not eaten anything.

The bell above the door dinged, signaling a customer was entering. She glanced up and spotted Melanie and Juli, two of her best customers, strolling into her shop. She'd become acquainted with Melanie when she'd gotten saved and started attending church regularly. Juli was the pastor's wife. Both of the women smiled as they approached the counter. "Girl, we missed you at church yesterday." Melanie looked tired. Dark circles were beneath her eyes. Her flawless nut-brown skin was not covered with makeup.

Juli nodded. "I was going to give you a call to check up on you but we decided to visit you instead."

Oh, both of these women were a sight for sore eyes. Juli sported a new short stylish cut. Her salt and pepper hair looked flattering against her medium brown skin. Juli always had been wise and kind – often giving well needed advice. She certainly needed advice right now.

She eyed her assistant. "Brooke I'm going to sit and have lunch with Melanie and Juli. Come get me if you need anything."

Brooke gave Raquel a mock salute. "Sure thing boss."

"Come on ladies, let's have some lunch." Juli and Melanie always ordered the same thing for lunch. So, she didn't need to ask them what they wanted. After she'd placed the tuna fish sandwiches, chips, fruit salad and steaming mugs of coffee on the table the threesome sat down.

Juli glanced at both of them. "I'll say grace unless one of you wants to do it."

Grace. She'd been praying so much over the last two weeks that she was sure that God was sick of hearing from her. Yeah, she had faith but still felt as if she were stumbling. She needed to be lifted up before the Lord. She took Juli's hand. "Yes, please say grace if you don't mind."

They bowed their heads.

"Lord, please be with Melanie as she goes through a rough time in her life. Please be with Melanie's cousin Chloe. That young girl has a tough road ahead of her but her dependence on you will give her strength. Lord, also, please be with Drake. That young man is lost and he has so much to learn if he's ever going to be a part of Chloe's life. Please be with Kyle Baxter, Lord. Kyle is battling a lot and I hope and pray that both Melanie and Kyle work through their problems. Kyle has found out some news about his parentage – hopefully this new-found information will help Kyle as he continues with his vacation. And, Lord, please let your Holy Spirit be with Raquel. Right before we entered the coffeeshop I looked through the window and noticed she looked a bit sad. We missed her at church the other day. Melanie and I want to be here for her as a friend. Thank you, Lord Jesus for this wonderful day and for this tasty food. Amen."

"Amen." Both Melanie and Raquel spoke simultaneously as they released their joined hands.

Juli's prayers were always heartfelt and longwinded. Today's prayer raised questions in her mind. She had no idea about most of the people she'd mentioned. Chloe was Melanie's cousin. She knew that Chloe had been giving Melanie problems lately. Melanie's herb shop was funded by Chloe's dad – but the price was steep. Melanie had to mentor her wayward cousin and she knew that it had taken a toll on her. "Who are Drake and Kyle?"

Melanie briefly grabbed Raquel's hand. "Girl, so much has happened over the last few weeks. I had to go on a road trip during the snowstorm to get Chloe. She ran away."

She raised her eyebrows. "What? Are you serious?"

Melanie nodded as she sipped her coffee. "It's been so stressful."

She could imagine – especially since Melanie was dealing with troublesome Chloe. "I went on a road trip too. I learned a lot – that's why I've been feeling so down lately. Tell me about your road trip first."

As they feasted on lunch Melanie brought Raquel up to speed about all that had gone on in her life. She told about Kyle, a man who was now vacationing across the street from her herb shop. She had a massive crush on Kyle – but discovered that Kyle was still battling with keeping his sobriety. "Let me show you what he looks like." She removed her phone from her purse and accessed her photos. "This is Kyle."

Raquel stared at the handsome brown-skinned man. He looked gorgeous. His dreamy, intense brown eyes and sculpted lips...she could understand why Melanie was so attracted to him. "Oh, Melanie, he's easy on the eyes."

All of them laughed just as Raquel glanced out the window. The man who she'd just seen in the photo stood outside blatantly staring at Melanie through the window. He appeared intense, sad, and somewhat lost. She grabbed Melanie's hand, about to tell her that Kyle was outside staring at her, when he stormed away. Looked like he didn't want Melanie to know that he was gawking at her like a lovesick teenager.

"What is it, Raquel?" Melanie glanced down just as Raquel released her hand. "Looks like you're upset or excited about something."

"Kyle was staring at you through the window a few seconds ago. He looked lovesick."

Juli grinned. "Melanie, give the poor man a chance. He really likes you and I think he'll be fair and honest with you. As I mentioned to you before, the man loves Jesus – so that's a good stepping stone for any relationship."

Melanie nodded as she seemed to ponder Juli's advice for a few minutes. After she'd finished her fruit salad it took Melanie an hour to tell all that had gone on during her road trip with Kyle. "Chloe ran away with her no-good boyfriend Drake. Since I can't seem to control her – her dad, my Uncle Larry, decided to pull the plug on our deal." When she'd first opened her herb shop Melanie had told Raquel that her Uncle Larry funded the shop as long as she agreed to mentor Chloe. Chloe was twenty-one years old but acted like she was still in high school.

Her breath caught. "Oh, Melanie. Does this mean that you won't be able to run your herb shop anymore?"

She slowly nodded as she opened her bag of potato chips. "I'm sad but glad at the same time. I really love running my herb shop but keeping an eye on Chloe was hard. She needs more time and guidance than I can provide. She's moved back home with Uncle Larry. He said that I could stay through the New Year. After that I need to decide what I'm going to do. I'll probably find a job and move back to Annapolis."

"Oh, I'm so sorry to hear that. I'll miss you so much."

"I'll miss you too girl. Let's try to spend as much time together as we can during the holidays. Deal?"

"Deal."

Juli topped off her coffee cup. "Now tell us about your road trip Raquel."

She told them all that had happened over the last two weeks. After describing the initial phone call from Ama she relayed how Patrick showed up. It took her over an hour to tell all about the last few weeks of her life. She told about her father's illness, his miraculous recovery, and about her growing feelings for Patrick. She didn't tell them about Patrick's mom's suicide – that wasn't something that she was at liberty to speak about. However, she did mention that Patrick had kept a secret from her – and she wondered if he had other secrets that he battled to share with her. Once she was finished talking the coffee shop had emptied. She certainly hadn't planned on visiting with Juli and Melanie for the entire afternoon, but she was glad that she was able to do so.

Juli patted Raquel's arm. "Oh, honey, I can't even begin to imagine how much of a shock that was – finding out that your father is still alive."

"I'm getting used to the idea slowly. I still can't seem to forgive him."

Melanie nodded. "I can understand your anger. Why don't you look up some scriptures about forgiveness if you haven't already done that. A few years ago I was angry about something and I just kept reciting forgiveness scriptures over and over again."

She'd not thought to do that. "I'll try that. Thank you."

Juli checked her watch. "I'd not planned on visiting so long. Spending time with the two of you this afternoon has been a blessing, but I must get home to start dinner."

"I have to go as well." Melanie stood up and started putting her coat on and Juli did the same. The threesome shared a group hug.

Juli looked directly into Raquel's eyes. "You keep me posted about your journey to forgiveness. If you need to talk to me about anything then call or text me."

"You can reach out to me anytime, too," Melanie piped in. "As far as Patrick is concerned, I think the two of you should take it slow. After you meet up with him on Christmas day you can talk to him on the phone once a day. Develop a rapport with him. Maybe spend time with him after church each Sunday. Then see what happens from there."

As she boxed up the leftover Butterscotch Bliss Buns to take to the community soup kitchen she gave Juli's and Melanie's advice deep thought.

Chapter 12

Patrick yawned. He eyed the time on his laptop. 8:30 PM. He'd been in the office for over twelve hours. He sighed. These long working hours had been atrocious. To top it all off, he'd overheard some of his coworkers gossiping. They'd implied that he'd be treated favorably since he was the boss's son.

He gritted his teeth with anger. Nothing could be further from the truth. Couldn't they see that? He'd not been working here for long. He was already working more hours than most of the staff members. If anything, his dad was treating him *harder* than most of the other workers. The spreadsheets, the numbers...depreciation, fixed assets, investments. *Lord, I'm tired of all of this.* He should be grateful that his father had provided a well-paying job in the accounting-finance profession. Yet, he didn't feel so grateful.

He just felt tired. One of the neighbors in his apartment complex had mentioned that he looked tired. He *felt* tired. He just wanted to let go and unwind and feel good. But, this job was crippling the life out of him. He missed Raquel so much. He just wanted to sit in front of a roaring fire and just hold her all night. Kiss her. His skin heated as he thought of all he'd like to do with Raquel. He pushed the wanton thoughts away.

He needed a little pick-me-up as he tried to finish up the cost analysis reports for the next meeting with his dad and the rest of the staff. He got up to stretch his legs and walked over to the windowsill and lifted his thermos and unscrewed the top. The delicious scent of chocolate and cinnamon calmed his frazzled nerves. His father's assistant thoughtfully provided a large vat of hot chocolate, as well as gingerbread cookies, for the staff to enjoy. The hot chocolate and the cookies were homemade.

Since he'd been in meetings all day, one of the staff members had saved him some hot chocolate in his thermos and had saved him some cookies. A blessing that someone had saved some for him before it was all gone. He plopped back into his chair and selected one of the gingerbread men from the plastic container. He bit into the cookie. So good. He loved the taste of ginger and cinnamon. He devoured all six of the cookies in minutes. He should've eaten dinner before eating so many cookies, but, he just couldn't resist. Everybody kept saying how good the treats tasted so he was anxious to try them. He took a huge sip of the hot chocolate.

He sighed with pleasure. The spicy sugary chocolate drink was amazing. Staring out the window, he thought about Raquel. He'd seen her from a distance while he'd been on his way to work the other day. He'd wanted to call out to her but he resisted. She looked as beautiful as ever. Back when they were dating, he'd not yet accepted Christ, so, they spent a lot of evenings together. When she used to spend the night at his house, she would always bake something for him. His favorite had been her gingerbread cookies.

He grinned, recalling how he'd first met her. He'd been outside doing his daily run and had spotted her sitting on a bench in the park.

Her head was usually down, either reading a book or looking at her phone. At times, he'd catch her staring at the birds in the trees. Her nut-brown skin and long dread-locked hair made him want to stop running and just stare. With her sultry good looks, he figured she had a boyfriend. He'd initially hesitated about approaching her since he wasn't sure if she'd be open to going out on a date with a white person.

One day, he went on his run earlier than usual. That's when he realized that she usually took a long walk around the park. When he spotted her on the bench, she was usually resting after her walk. He changed his routine, took a walk instead, at the same time she was walking. He struck up a conversation with her and from there, things had gone smoothly. She had a passion for food and cooking. Unhappy with her job as an executive assistant, she'd shared her dream of owning her own coffee shop. He enjoyed the great food that she prepared. Being with her was so relaxing.

"Patrick? You okay?" His dad strolled into the office.

No, he wasn't okay. He missed Raquel and was tired from working so many hours. He could barely think his brain was so tired. He couldn't voice his disgruntlement about his job to his dad. His dad worked long hours too. He wondered if his dad's wife, Gretchen, ever argued with him about being away from home since he worked so much overtime. He shut down his computer. He just didn't have the energy to continue working tonight.

His dad spotted the crumbs on the napkin and the thermos of hot chocolate. "Looks like you got some of the cookies and hot chocolate."

"Yeah, it was good."

His father pushed an office chair over to the window near his son. He eased into the chair. "You were quiet today. You didn't seem to be paying attention during the meetings."

"Dad. I'm sorry. Seeing Raquel again rattled me. Been thinking about her all day."

"But that's one reason why you came back. You wanted to see her again and figure things out." His father clapped him on the shoulder. "I hope things work out." Patrick nodded as they continued to stare out the window. "You sure you want to stay here by yourself for Christmas?"

Christmas was coming up and he didn't know how he'd wait before seeing Raquel again. "Don't worry about me. I'm good."

"What about your sisters?"

"They've made plans to spend Christmas with their friends from college."

His dad nodded. "I see." He paused. "Well, you know Gretchen says you're more than welcome to join us."

His father had remarried ten years ago. His wife, Gretchen, was nice enough. But he really didn't feel like imposing on their vacation. Gretchen had three adult kids from her previous marriage. Her children, their spouses, and her grandchildren were meeting up at a luxurious log cabin in Aspen Colorado during Christmas week. His dad was looking forward to the vacation and really wanted him to come along. He didn't know Gretchen's kids very well and he honestly didn't feel like going. He didn't feel like socializing with a bunch of strangers for the entire week.

He was kind of hoping he and his dad could go fishing, alone, in the spring, just as they did in Ireland, when he was a young boy. Those were some of the happiest times of his life – back before his mother's depression got worse.

"Don't worry about me. I'll be fine."

"Ok. I'll stop mentioning it." He sighed and took a deep breath. "By the way, I set up a meeting with some new investors. I wanted to make sure the meeting was on your calendar." He recited the date and time of the meeting.

Patrick stood up and rushed to his desk. His desk was a mess of papers. He pushed the papers aside, mumbling to himself.

"Something wrong?"

"My phone. I had it this morning. I couldn't find it earlier during our meetings. I thought I'd left it here in my office." He was going to use the phone to add the meeting to his schedule. Maybe the phone was in his car. He'd been so tired lately – and when we was really tired he could be forgetful. He didn't want to forget to add this important meeting to his schedule. He stifled a yawn. "I'm sure it's in my car. I'll see you tomorrow, Dad."

He rushed from the office and ran down the two flights of stairs. *Update my phone. Update my phone.* He chanted this to himself so that he wouldn't forget to add the meeting as soon as he found his phone. He yawned, eyes closed, as he stormed out of the building and collided with someone. His eyes jerked open as soon as wet heated warmth exploded onto his shirt. "Ouch." The hot coffee sizzled his frigid torso.

"Patrick." Raquel's shocked voice echoed in the cold frosty air.

He couldn't believe that he'd just slammed into Raquel and made her spill her coffee. "Raquel, I'm so sorry."

Her coffee cup had been smashed so she threw it into the trash bin. "That's okay. It's too late to be drinking coffee anyway."

He eyed her entire body. She looked great. The urge to kiss her suddenly consumed him. He pushed the thought aside. He wondered if she'd missed him. In spite of his overloaded work schedule, he missed her so much. He thought that working hard would help him to not think about her too much since Christmas was still days away.

Just the opposite happened. She haunted his dreams. He honestly didn't think that he could wait until Christmas to see her again. "Where are you going in such a hurry?"

Oh, that's right. He needed to get to his phone before he forgot. "I'm going to my car. It's right over here. I can give you a ride home if you want."

He mentally sighed with relief when she followed him to his vehicle. He unlocked the car. Thank God! His phone was nestled in the cup holder. He quickly added the meeting to his calendar before focusing on Raquel again. Since he'd ruined her cup of coffee he wanted to invite her to his place for a night cap. No. Bad idea. Being alone with Raquel at night, right next to his empty bedroom, was a recipe for fornication. "Can I buy you another cup of coffee?"

She shook her head. "I'm fine."

He didn't want to drop her off at home. He wanted to talk to her. He gestured toward a path leading to the beach. "Do you mind if we sit for a minute? I wanted to talk to you."

She hesitated. Oh no, looked like she was going to say no. He sighed when she finally nodded. They walked the short path and sat on a bench. All of the snow had melted and the air was a cold thirty-five degrees. A hamburger joint that was located behind the bench was still open. The lights from the restaurant spilled onto the bench. The scent of fried meat and grilled onions mingled with the frosty ocean air. His stomach rumbled. He'd not had dinner tonight. He didn't count the cookies that he ate as dinner.

"Sounds like you're hungry."

"Aye. Haven't had dinner yet. Do you mind if we go in and get a burger?"

"Sounds good. I haven't eaten dinner yet either."

He pushed the door open for her to enter the restaurant. A large Christmas tree nestled in the corner. Multicolored lights blinked from the branches. Several wrapped gifts were arranged in a neat circle beneath the evergreen. Christmas carols belted from the sound system. A family dined at one of the tables. The youngsters jabbered about Santa's upcoming visit.

They ordered at the counter and sat at a table near the window. His stomach rumbled again. Raquel chuckled as she removed her gloves. "Why haven't you eaten dinner yet?" She peered at him. "You look tired. Didn't you sleep well last night?"

Sure, he'd slept. He'd been dreaming about her every night since they'd returned but he didn't want to let her know that. "I'm exhausted from working so much. Sometimes I worry about working for my dad. Makes it hard for me to sleep sometimes."

"You're exhausted and you can't sleep?" She reached over and took his hand. She squeezed his fingers. "Sounds like you need to find another job."

No way could he do that. "I need to work for my dad."

Their server approached with two thick cheeseburgers, golden fries, and soft drinks. Once the worker had left Raquel squeezed his hand. "I'll say grace." They bowed their heads. "Lord, please be with Patrick. Help him to find a job that's fulfilling and uses his best talents. Lord, please be with me as I continue to try to forgive my dad. His recovery is a blessing, and please, if it's Your will, continue to help him heal. And, thank you Lord for this wonderful meal. Sharing a meal with Patrick this evening is an unexpected blessing. Amen."

"Amen." Eating with him was a blessing? How thoughtful of her to mention that. He bit into the burger. Thick gooey cheese, fried onions, and seasoned meat created a symphony of pleasure in his mouth. He wanted to ask Raquel more questions but was too hungry to focus on that right now. He'd ask her after he'd enjoyed his meal. He dunked the crisp hot salty fries in a puddle of ketchup. He chased his meal down with his soft drink. The cool sweetness of the beverage was the perfect end to the meal. He sighed. Unable to resist, he returned to the counter and ordered dessert. Minutes later their server returned with two hot slices of apple pie with ice cream.

Raquel had just finished her burger. "I didn't tell you to order dessert for me."

He shrugged. If Raquel didn't want it, he could easily eat it. "You don't have to eat it if you don't want to."

She giggled. "I can't pass up apple pie a la mode."

He loved their apple pie. The restaurant had a sign hanging near the counter bragging about their homemade apple pie. The hot sweet cinnamon apples and flaky crust contrasted perfectly with the cold vanilla ice cream. Once he was done with the pie he sighed with pleasure. He stifled a yawn. Again, he wished that he could take Raquel back to his place. He pushed the wanton thought away as he focused on her.

Should he hold her hand? No, he didn't want to push it. At least she'd agreed to talk to him. "Where were you walking when I bumped into you earlier?"

"Back home. I just left my friend Melanie's. She hosted Bible study tonight."

"Oh. You shouldn't be walking home by yourself at night."

"Melanie offered to drive me, but I wanted to walk. I have a lot on my mind and walking helps me to think. I told her that I'd call her as soon as I got home." She pulled her phone out of her purse and sent a text. He assumed she was texting Melanie to let her know that she'd be home soon.

"What did you talk about at Bible study?"

"Forgiveness. I needed to talk about that. As I said, I'm still struggling to forgive my dad."

"You talk to him since you came back home?"

She shook her head. "I call Ama often and chat with her. She lets him know that I've called."

"These things take time, Rocky. You're trying to forgive him. That's what's important. Forgiveness can be a journey." He eyed her while she sipped her soft drink. "Why did you pray about me finding a job using my talents?"

She plopped her soda onto the table and took a deep breath. "You're exhausted working for your dad. You just said so."

"But I need to work for him."

"I know you want to get closer to your dad. But, maybe working for him is a bad idea. I remember when we were dating years ago, you were working in accounting and finance then, too. You'd complain about the long hours, especially during tax season."

"Raquel, a lot of people complain about their jobs. There are things to like and dislike about all occupations." It almost sounded like she didn't want him to have a better relationship with his father. He couldn't imagine her feeling like that so he must be missing something.

She nodded, her dreadlocks swaying with the movement. "I know that. But, you seldom mentioned anything that you *liked* about your job. You only mention what you *don't* like."

He threw his hands into the air. "So?" Hopefully she'd make her point. Since he'd eaten his fatigue had gotten worse and he just wanted to lie down. He sensed an argument brewing, and he didn't have the energy to fight with Raquel right now.

She stalled for a few seconds and took a sip of her drink. "You need to follow your dreams just as I have with my coffee shop." She took his hand and squeezed his fingers. Her soft brown hand contrasted with his pale skin. "It's always bothered you that your relationship with your father fell apart when he moved back to the states. You've been working yourself ragged, making choices that would please *him* instead of making choices that will please *you*."

He pulled his hand away. No way did she know what she was talking about. "What do you mean?"

"You have undergraduate and graduate degrees in accounting and finance. You probably knew that your dad would approve of that choice which is probably why you picked it. When you were able to work alongside your dad – when that opportunity came up – you lunged at it. Patrick, you're hurt and you want your dad's approval. You want the same love he had for you when you were a kid." She took another deep breath. "But working yourself ragged trying to please him, and being miserable yourself, is not helpful." He gritted his teeth. Raquel thought she was so smart, as if she knew everything about him. But, she didn't know. He was doing what he had to do. "Don't be angry with me. Let me finish."

He waited a bit before giving her a curt nod so that she could continue. "Patrick, you're happiest when you're helping teenagers. You used to thrive when you did your coaching on the weekends at the community center. You even bonded with Buddy and Judith over video games. I think you'd make an awesome teacher. You could even try and be a coach or a physical education teacher at a high school." She shrugged. "Follow your passion. You'll be a lot happier."

He winced. "I never said I was unhappy."

She grabbed his hand again. "Talk to your dad. Have you ever told him how you felt? Have you ever told him how you struggle to understand why your relationship hasn't been the same since you were a kid?" His dad never wanted to talk about anything with him besides business matters. They rarely spoke of the time they'd spent together before he'd divorced his mum.

"I need to get home. I have a long day tomorrow." No way did he even have the courage or the energy to *think* about changing his profession. He couldn't even imagine telling his dad exactly how he felt. If he did, would that ruin the somewhat tenuous relationship they currently had?

They put on their coats and left the restaurant and walked the short distance to his car. Both of them were silent during the short drive to Raquel's house. Christmas lights winked from her windows. A huge green wreath decorated her front door. He didn't bother exiting to open her car door for her. She rushed from his vehicle, unlocked her front door, and went into her house.

Chapter 13

E *phesians 4:32*

Be kind and compassionate to one another, forgiving each other, just as in Christ God forgave you.

Raquel mentally recited the Bible verse as she put on her sweatshirt and jeans. The day had gotten a tad bit warm – almost sixty degrees. Instead of boots she shoved her feet into a pair of sneakers. After donning a light jacket, she exited her house and locked the door.

As she walked to Melanie's for lunch she relished the warm sunshine on her face. Brooke had agreed to man the coffee shop for the day. Raquel needed a day off from work as she sorted through her problems. About fifteen minutes later as she approached Melanie's house, she happened to look at the house across the street. The same man she'd seen gawking at Melanie at the coffee shop...Kyle, wasn't that his name? He stood peeking out the window – looking at Melanie's house. Looked like he wanted to get a glimpse of Melanie. Unable to resist, she smiled and waved. His eyes widened with surprise as he gave her a small tentative wave back.

She knocked on Melanie's door. Melanie opened the door and pulled her into a hug. "Hey Raquel."

She hugged her back. The garbled sound of....why that sounded like children? A loud scream followed by the sound of angst filtered from the living room. What in the world?

"Come on in. Sorry about the noise. My friends Karen and Keith are visiting Kyle for Christmas. I invited Karen and her twin boys over for lunch. I hope you don't mind them joining us." She recalled that Melanie had mentioned that she'd grown up with the identical twins - Keith and Kyle. She'd had a crush on Keith for years. But she'd never seriously dated him. Keith married Karen. She found out recently that Kyle had had a secret crush on Melanie for years but hadn't shown his true feelings until recently.

Before she entered the kitchen she grabbed Melanie's hand. "Speaking of Kyle, I saw him gawking at your house a few minutes ago. He was peeking through the window."

Melanie rolled her eyes. "Yeah, I'm not surprised."

"You said you really like him."

"I do like him. A lot. I also appreciate all that he's done to help me since he's been on his Christmas vacation. But girl, he's got so many problems. I told him I had to think about dating him. I might have already mentioned that we're meeting up on Christmas day – just like you and Patrick."

When she entered the kitchen she spotted a petite brown-skinned woman cutting up sandwiches into bite sized pieces. Two identical toddlers were strapped to the kitchen chairs in some sort of child-protection seat. She assumed this was used since Melanie didn't have highchairs at her house. One of the twins looked over at her and grinned and waved. Drool ran down the side of his mouth as he munched on a piece of sandwich.

She smiled at the toddler. "Hello there." The other twin didn't seem to be as friendly. He just munched on a piece of his sandwich and stared at her.

"I'm Karen. So glad to meet you." Instead of shaking hands, the woman gave her a warm hug. Surprising since she didn't know Karen at all. She returned her hug.

"It's nice to meet you too Karen."

After they were all seated and had said grace Melanie served lunch. She served tuna salad sandwiches, homemade potato chips and home-made lemonade. Wow, excitement bubbled within her when she spot-ted the food. Melanie's tuna fish was the best. She bit into the soft sandwich. The tuna was loaded with jalapenos. So good and spicy. It paired nicely with the crunchy salty homemade potato chips. After drinking two large glasses of lemonade she enjoyed strawberry gelatin with whipped cream for dessert.

Raquel leaned back and patted her full stomach. "That was deli-cious. Thanks so much."

"It was delicious." Karen agreed as she drained her glass of lemon-ade.

"I wanted to ask you all about something." Raquel then told them about her conversation with Patrick the previous evening. "I think he's mad at me. After what I said last night he might not want to meet up with me on Christmas."

Karen patted her shoulder. The twins were taking a nap on a blan-ket in the living room so it was a blessing that they could have a conversation without interruptions. "You know, Raquel, sometimes it's hard for people to see the truth about themselves. Just give him some time. You said he was exhausted. Maybe after he's rested up the two of you can talk about it rationally."

Might as well tell them all of her doubts. "He seemed so upset. I wonder if he's going to show up on Christmas day."

Melanie shook her head. "Oh, Raquel. I highly doubt that he'd stand you up. I think he'll come. I'm sure if he's unable to make it, or if he changes his mind, he'll let you know." She paused for a few minutes. "Have you spoken to your dad yet?"

Not surprising that Melanie asked her about that. "I'm still struggling with that. I still recite scriptures to myself and I speak to his wife. Ama knows about my struggle."

"Raquel, Melanie told me about your dad. It's a blessing that he was healed and that he's getting better. I'm sorry to hear that he treated your mom so terribly. If someone were to abuse my mom like that I'd struggle to forgive them. So I don't blame you for feeling as you do."

Nice knowing that Karen sympathized with how she felt. Outside of reciting scriptures and prayers she wasn't sure what else she could do. How could you *make* yourself forgive someone if you didn't feel that forgiveness in your heart? "I just keep thinking about what he did to hurt my mom."

Melanie sat up straighter in her chair. Her eyes sparkled with warmth – looked like she'd come up with a suggestion to help her. "Why don't you break that cycle?"

"Huh?" She had no idea what Melanie was talking about.

"You said you've been speaking to Ama everyday about your father's health, right?"

"Yes..." She still didn't understand what Melanie was getting at.

"Well, why don't you ask her what your father was like since they've been married? Find out more about him. What happened to him after he got out of prison? Focus on the changes he may have made in his life instead of what he did to your mom."

"Hmm..." Melanie's advice gave her something to think about.

Wanting to know Karen better, Raquel asked her questions about her relationship with her husband Keith. She wondered how they met and how long they'd been married.

About an hour later the twins woke up. One of them cried. Karen went into the living room and changed their diapers and then she placed them into their stroller. She returned to the kitchen. "I need to be heading back across the street now. Thanks so much for hosting lunch Melanie. When you return to Annapolis we can do this again. Raquel it was nice meeting you. If you're ever in Annapolis please visit."

Raquel hugged Melanie and Karen before gathering her purse and the leftover tuna fish that Melanie had insisted that she take home with her.

While she strolled back to her house, she enjoyed the semi-warm sunshine. She walked quickly as she thought about Melanie's advice about her father. As soon as she entered her house she dumped the leftover food into the kitchen before rummaging in her purse for her phone. She immediately called Ama. "Hi, Raquel." She gave Raquel the usual rundown about her father's health.

"Ama I wanted to know more about my dad."

"What do you mean, child?"

"I keep focusing on how much he hurt my mom."

"Yeah. Go on."

"Well, what are some good things that he's done? Did you meet up shortly after he got out of prison?"

"I met your father at church about a year after he'd gotten out of prison. He was able to find work as a handyman. It was difficult for him to find regular employment at an office job due to his prison record." She took a deep breath. "What I love most about your father is his compassion for others."

She patiently waited for Ama to continue.

"To make some extra money a man at our church owned an ice cream truck. He hired your father to work the ice cream truck part time. Your dad went to some poor neighborhoods. He used his own money to pay for ice cream that he'd give away free to kids. The truck also had a compartment for hot foods. He'd wanted to give away heated foods to the kids too. But he simply couldn't afford it. He wasn't making much of a salary from this part-time job since he was using the money he made to pay for the ice cream." Ama paused and took a deep breath. "The man at our church who owned the ice cream truck died. Your father inherited the truck. Someone else at our church advised him about how to make himself into a non-profit that provided food to kids in poor neighborhoods. People donated food and ice cream to his ministry."

Warmth filled her soul like hot fudge as she thought about her father ministering to others. "My dad did all of that?"

"Yes child."

"Who runs the truck now?"

"One of our church members runs it. You know, if you Google his name you might find some newspaper articles that feature his ministry. Your dad hated seeing kids go hungry. The summer was worse because these kids used to get free meals at school each weekday. But when the schools were closed for the summer – that was one source of food that was taken away from them – and it hurt. They used to look forward to seeing your dad come around with free food."

After she rang off with Ama she Googled her dad's name. She found a few newspaper articles that featured his ministry. There were several pictures of him beside his ice cream/food truck serving needy children. *Oh Lord. Thanks for allowing me to find out this informa-*

tion. Such a blessing that my father was able to minister to these sweet young children.

After bookmarking and saving the articles she pulled the curtain open and glanced outside. It had grown completely dark and silver stars dotted the inky sky. Longing welled up inside of her. She wanted to see Patrick so bad that it ached. Fisting the curtain she wondered what would happen if she called him and told him about the newspaper articles.

No, that would be a bad idea. He was still mad at her for what she'd said about his pursuing his dreams. Perhaps she could text him?

Not a good idea. It was probably best that they meet up on Christmas day just as they'd planned. She sighed as she dropped the curtain. Uneasiness swept through her like a tidal wave as she leaned back into the living room chair and closed her eyes. "Lord, what am I going to do if Patrick doesn't show up for our Christmas date?"

Chapter 14

Patrick eyed Raquel as she made a beeline for the back door of the church. The special mid-week Christmas cantata/church service had just ended. She was one of the first people out the door. Yep, she was probably in a hurry because she didn't want to talk to him. As he slowly ambled toward the exit along with the rest of the church he couldn't help but think about what had occurred since Raquel had told him to follow his dreams. He absentmindedly said 'Merry Christmas' to the church members who spoke to him, still in deep thought.

He'd once entertained the idea of becoming a schoolteacher, but then he'd nixed it. He imagined his father wouldn't have been proud of him. He doubted his dad would've disapproved but, he still figured that he'd be somewhat disappointed.

And he didn't want to disappoint his dad.

What was weird was, he'd never told Raquel about his dreams of becoming a high school teacher. But, she *knew* him. He couldn't fault her for making him see the truth of his actions. After much reflection he realized he still ached for his father's approval – at this rate – it looked like he'd never receive it. He stifled a yawn. He'd been working so much overtime. All he wanted to do was go home and take a long nap – but he had to go into the office to finish another project. He'd left the office on time that day to attend church. Who returned to the office at eight o'clock at night to work on a report about research and development costs? When would these long work hours ever end?

As he slowly exited the church with the rest of the crowd, he bumped into someone. "Patrick. Merry Christmas."

"Merry Christmas." It took him a minute to remember the man's name. Ah, Mr. Evans. He was in charge of the outreach program at the community center. "Mr. Evans. It's been a while since I've seen you." Since their congregation was so large he supposed they'd never managed to run into each other after service before.

The two men shook hands. Mr. Evans scratched the top of his salt-and-pepper hair, his eyebrows raised. "I'd heard you were back in town. You were one of our best volunteers when you used to live here. I was disappointed that you didn't sign up to volunteer when you returned to the Outer Banks."

As they made their way to the parking lot Patrick peered at the older man. His brown skin had a few wrinkles and he'd mentioned his grandchildren a few times. He recalled Mr. Evans being kind and thoughtful. Right now he needed someone to talk to. He didn't want Mr. Evans to think that he wasn't interested in helping out at the community center. "Are you busy right now Mr. Evans?"

"No. Did you need something?"

He took a deep breath and nodded. "I wanted to talk to you about why I've not been volunteering at the community center. Do you want to have a late dinner at the Chinese restaurant across the street? My treat."

The older man grinned, showing his perfect white teeth. "I'm never one to turn down a free meal. My wife is out of town. So, I don't need to rush home."

He mentally sighed with relief. Great. Maybe talking to Mr. Evans would help him to make the right decision about his plight. They entered the restaurant and were seated at a table with an ocean view. After placing orders for sweet and sour chicken, egg rolls, and Cokes, Patrick cleared his throat. Hopefully Mr. Evans wouldn't get too bored with all he was about to share with him. Briefly he again recalled all of the work he needed to do at the office. He pushed the thought away.

Once their food was served and they'd blessed the meal, Patrick reminded Mr. Evans about Raquel. "I was dating her before my mum passed."

The man nodded. "Yes, I remember seeing her at the community center. She once mentioned to me that you'd probably be happier working at the community center full time instead of crunching numbers all day."

He almost choked on his bite of eggroll he was so surprised. He took a swig of Coke. "She said that?"

"Yeah. Pretty woman. I could tell that she adored you. When I see her at church she always says hi."

While they continued eating he told of his return to Ireland because of his mum's death. He didn't mention his mum's suicide. He spoke of raising his sisters. Returning to the states to work with his dad and reconnecting with Raquel. He finished by telling him about his conversation with Raquel at the burger joint.

"Patrick, are you mad that Raquel is right? You obviously have issues with fixing your relationship with your father – but fixing that is beyond your control. Such a task involves two people. I feel that you need to talk to your father about everything – just as Raquel suggested.

Tell him how you feel and that you're tired from working so many hours. I'm sure your dad doesn't want you to suffer from burnout."

He wondered if his dad would even care if he burned out from working so much. "I suppose I could find another job. As far as Raquel being right – it's just strange that she could see something about myself that I wasn't able to openly admit."

"Well, that happens sometimes. It's hard to admit to our true feelings."

Although teaching sounded good, he figured he wasn't qualified. He had no teaching degree. He doubted teaching could match the salary his dad was currently paying.

"Patrick, have you ever thought about working for a private school?"

"I haven't researched working in the school system at all. At least not recently."

"Let me ask you this, are you a CPA?"

"Yes, I have my CPA license." Some had doubted that he had a CPA license since he was Irish. The CPA exam could only be taken by American citizens. He had to patiently explain to some that he had dual citizenship since his mum was Irish and his dad is American. "Why do you ask?"

"I work for Fishers of Men Christian School. Our controller, who is in charge of all of our accounting, is about to retire. Would you be interested in applying? I guarantee the hours would not be as along as what you are working now." He briefly mentioned the salary range.

He winced. He'd take a cut in salary. He supposed if he were hired he'd have his quality of life back. "I'd have free time to volunteer at the community center."

His heart skipped with dread when Mr. Evans shook his head. "You might be able to volunteer a little bit at the community center. What I failed to mention is you'd be working with the kids too."

This was a surprise. "Really? As the controller?" How or why would somebody in accounting interact with the students?

"No, as an assistant coach. Our current controller doubles as an assistant coach. I've seen you work with the kids in the community center. You'd be a good fit for the job and I'm sure the kids will respect and like you. I could let them know at tomorrow's staff meeting that you're interested and put in a good word for you. I'll email an application package to you as soon as I get home."

Whew. He'd not been expecting a conversation such as this to play out. He glanced at their empty plates. Their server approached and refilled their beverages. He leaned back into his chair and sighed. "I don't know what to say."

"You can apply. Pray about it first. At the very least I can let them know that you *might* be interested."

He closed his eyes for a few seconds and then finally nodded. "That sounds safe. Tell them that I might be interested and send me the application." He recited his email address and phone number. Mr. Evans placed the information into his phone.

After they ended their meal and shook hands Patrick couldn't go home. He needed to just walk around and think. He returned to the church and removed his sneakers from his trunk. He changed into his sneakers and walked to the cold dark deserted beach. The gentle waves lapped onto the frigid sandy shore. He strolled along the shore as he shoved his hands into his pockets.

He couldn't even bring himself to go to work that night he was so consumed with emotional turmoil. He loved Raquel and wanted to make things work between them. It was wrong for him to get upset when she'd given him her unsolicited advice. She'd only been sharing her honest opinion. If they were ever able to work things out and possibly get married then...he gulped, just thinking about being married to Raquel, made him pause – but pause in a good way. He sensed if she were a part of his life his life would be fuller, richer, even more enjoyable.

He continued walking as a gentle cold breeze blew. He took a deep breath and pulled out his phone and checked the time. He'd been walking for over an hour. He plopped onto a nearby bench and continued staring at the dark ocean while thinking.

Lord, I really need your help. If I quit working for my father, what will he think? Will he be upset? Angry? Will I destroy all chances of solidifying the relationship with my dad? What about Raquel, Lord? Will she be willing to have a relationship with me? I got mad at her for voicing her thoughts. What does she think about me? How does she feel about me? Amen. As he trudged back to his car he figured that he'd discover the answers to his questions soon.

That night, he tossed and turned in his sleep. He ended up throwing his blanket off and paced around his apartment – releasing pent up energy. He finally managed to get a few hours of sleep.

When he went to work the next morning, his dad rushed into his office. "Patrick, you didn't return to work last night to get a jump start on the profitability review report."

Fatigue weighed upon him like a thick heavy blanket, almost suffocating him. When he'd looked at himself in the mirror that morning, he'd looked tired and downtrodden. His life was a mess and he needed to do something about it. There was no reason that he should feel miserable. "I had some things that I had to take care of last night."

"You should place your job above all of your other obligations. I expect high dedication from all of my employees."

He just couldn't respond. When he remained silent his father turned and rushed away. He was probably going to go and fuss at somebody else for not working after hours. As he turned on his laptop and began analyzing spreadsheets his stomach rumbled with hunger. He'd not had anything to eat or drink this morning. He grabbed a bottle of water from the small refrigerator beneath his desk and opened it. He took a long drink. The cool liquid felt good going down his parched throat.

He wasn't going to be eating anything today. He was fasting. Maybe if he fasted he'd feel closer to the Lord and figure out how to fix his messed up life.

Chapter 15

Raquel hesitated before calling Ama. Her mind had been muddled with negative thoughts about her dad until she'd focused on all of the positive aspects of his life. Now, she needed to reach out to Ama to let her know that she'd like to speak to her father if he was able and willing. Not only had she been thinking about her dad.

She'd also been thinking about Patrick.

The other day at church she'd seen him enter the building before the cantata started. After the service she'd made a quick exit, not wanting to talk to him. She didn't know if he was still mad at her about what she'd said about his relationship with his dad. Later she'd spotted him having dinner with Mr. Evans at the Chinese restaurant. She'd been close enough to see the forlorn and pensive expression on his face. His shoulders were hunched. Looked like he had something important on his mind. Oh, how she hoped he wasn't having second thoughts about their Christmas meet-up.

Pushing thoughts of Patrick from her mind she finally called Ama.

"Good afternoon, child. How have you been?"

"Fine. How are you?"

"I've been okay. Your father's health has been getting better." Ama gave her a rundown on how much her father's health had improved.

"Is he sleeping right now?"

"No, he's awake. Just finished his lunch."

"Can I talk to him."

"Sure, child. I'll put you on speaker."

"Raquel?" Her dad's rough gravely voice echoed through the phone.

"Hi. How are you feeling?"

"Getting better each day, praise the Lord."

"That's good to hear." She took a deep breath. *Lord, please help me to say the right words.* "I wanted to know if I can start talking to you. Maybe come down to visit." She'd like to bring Patrick with her if he was willing to come.

"You were mighty upset the last time we talked." He coughed a bit. "But I understand your anger. I'm trying to get my life straight with God one day at a time."

"I forgive you. It's taken me a long time to learn how to forgive. Ama told me that you used to run an ice cream and food truck to feed disadvantaged kids. I read newspaper articles about you doing that. What a blessing you were to those children."

She smiled as her father seemed to relax as he told her all about how he'd started his ice cream truck ministry. As he continued talking, his voice became animated. She could do this, have a relationship with her dad. It might not be the same as a true father-daughter relationship since he'd not raised her. But she was sure it'd turn out to be a fruitful relationship regardless – as long as they kept Jesus as a part of their lives.

After she rang off with her dad she got comfortable in her living room chair. She stared out the window. Her life would be as close to perfect as possible on this God-given earth if she could now fix things with Patrick.

Christmas Eve

Patrick knocked on the open door of his dad's office. His father stood at the large bay window. His shoulders slumped as if he were sad or upset about something. Well, that was strange. Since his dad didn't seem to hear the knock he entered. "Dad?"

His dad's brow furrowed with confusion. "Oh, Patrick. I didn't realize we'd scheduled a meeting."

They hadn't. His heart thrummed. He gulped while clutching the dreaded piece of paper. His dad was kind of old fashioned. If you resigned, he wanted a piece of paper stating that you were resigning and *why* you were resigning. He'd heard that most people didn't do a paper resignation – they simply sent an email. But, he wanted to make his dad happy. To be sure everyone was informed, he'd be following up his resignation with an email.

He tried to wipe his sweaty palms on his pants, but, it was too late. Moisture had dripped into spots on the piece of paper. Drat. Oh well, it didn't matter. As long as his father accepted his resignation and was open to having a frank discussion with him, then a bit of wetness on the paper was nothing to stress over.

His dad seemed like he was in a weird mood. Perhaps he'd had a fight with his wife. He closed the door. Hopefully his father didn't have any other meetings or appointments lined up. He needed a bit of time to tell his father what was on his mind. "I wanted to talk to you about my position here."

Still frowning, his dad turned toward him. "What about it?"

He gently offered the paper to his father. "Read this please."

He scanned the document. His mouth dropped open. His blue eyes appeared startled as he looked directly at him. "You're leaving the company?" His voice came out low, modulated, as if he were trying to control his angry tone.

"Yes." *Lord help me.* "This isn't the right job for me. I need a job where I can enjoy my life outside of work." Since he'd not shared his future employment details in his resignation letter, he figured it was best to let his father know. "Starting the second week in January I'll be working as the controller at Fishers of Men. It's a private Christian all-boy high school. I'll also be an assistant coach. I like working with youth."

Again, the furrowed brow. His dad seemed confused. "But you're one of my best employees."

This was surprising. "You've never told me that before."

"I didn't think I had to."

"Dad your employees won't know that they're valued unless you tell them." A warm tingly feeling flowed through him – kind of like hot butterscotch over vanilla ice cream. Just hearing that he was a valued employee made him feel good. However, this wonderful feeling wasn't enough to change his mind about working for his dad.

His father cleared his throat. "I didn't know you enjoyed working with kids."

Well, looked like now was a good time to get everything off his chest. He gestured toward the table and chairs. "Mind if we sit for a minute?" He'd been so nervous that he'd momentarily forgotten that it was Christmas Eve. His father was being generous by allowing the staff to go home at one o'clock this afternoon.

As he plopped into a chair, he suddenly recalled something his dad had told him a while ago. "I thought you were going to be gone now.

Weren't you vacationing with Gretchen and her kids at a cabin for Christmas?" He couldn't even remember where his dad had said the cabin was located.

His father hung his head and stared at the carpet for several seconds. "Gretchen wants a divorce. We decided to spend Christmas apart. Gives us some time to think about everything."

Shock as thick as pea soup coursed through his veins. He gulped. That was definitely something that he'd not been expecting to hear. "Dad. I'm sorry. Anything I can do?"

He shook his head. "No. Gretchen wants us to go to counseling." He sighed. "So far, I've refused."

He shrugged. "It's none of my business...but, you seem sad right now. If you want to save your marriage, then maybe you can try to do what Gretchen asks."

"Maybe."

"This probably isn't the best time to talk about this but...well it's eating at me and if I don't say something about it - it will continue to bother me."

"What is it?"

"I miss spending time with you Dad. When I was a kid just you and I would go fishing and it was fun. After the divorce things changed. You acted like you didn't want to be a father to me anymore. I want to reconnect with you again. Maybe go on a weekend fishing trip." He took a deep breath. "You didn't know that I enjoyed working with youth because you don't *know* me. I'd like for you to know me as a person – as your son. Not just as somebody who works for you."

His dad remained silent for several minutes. Patrick wondered if he should leave the room to give his father some privacy. His dad finally nodded. "I'd like that Patrick. After your mom – well after the divorce – just being around you reminded me of a painful situation. I should've handled things differently and I'm sorry. We can talk about it as we spend time together."

He suddenly had a wonderful idea. He'd been worried about his visit with Raquel at her house the following day. Well, looked like he'd found a solution. "Dad, what are you doing tomorrow for Christmas?"

Chapter 16

R aquel opened her eyes and rolled toward her bedstand. She checked her phone. Five o'clock AM. Hopefully Patrick was still coming for their Christmas meet-up. She probably should have double checked but, for some reason, she felt that she should just leave it in the Lord's hands.

After enjoying a hot cup of coffee and some toast she read her devotional. She then fried up celery and onions and baked a pan of cornbread. She needed those ingredients to make her tasty cornbread stuffing. Once she'd prepared the stuffing she removed the Cornish game hens from the fridge. She'd initially figured that two game hens would be enough for the both of them. Then for some reason, she'd gotten a third one, just in case she wanted leftovers for the next few days.

She turned on some Christmas music and started the mashed potatoes and gravy while the hens cooked. She'd already made dessert the previous day. Sweet potato pie with fresh whipped cream. Once the food had been prepared, she returned to her bedroom and showered and changed into her fetching red dress and slip on pumps. Butterflies floated through her stomach. *Lord, please help me to not be nervous.* Once she was ready, she returned to the living room and plugged in her Christmas tree. The glow of the lights against the pretty greenery caused a warm tingly feeling to emerge all over herself. She smiled as she continued to enjoy the festive décor. She closed her eyes as thoughts of her mom filtered through her mind. They'd spent so many wonderful Christmases together – baking, fellowshipping and just having wonderful times. *Oh Lord, how I miss my mom.* She swiped away the sudden tears from her cheeks. She took a deep breath. The tears weren't sad. Her feelings were bittersweet. A gentle cleansing feeling filled her soul. *Lord, I feel so refreshed right now.* She suddenly recalled that she needed to phone Ama and her dad later that day to wish them a Merry Christmas. She jerked as soon as her phone dinged with a text. Hopefully Patrick wasn't texting her to cancel. The text was from Melanie. She breathed a sigh of relief.

Met up with Kyle for breakfast early this morning.

We're going to start dating! I'm so excited about spending time with him!

Her text went on to describe how handsome Kyle had looked in his suit and tie. She also mentioned that he'd made a huge batch of rocky road candy for them to enjoy. Mclanie had told her that Kyle found candy making therapeutic. He'd learned to do it in rehab.

She jumped at the loud knock at her front door. Still trying to calm her racing heart she quickly strolled to the door and opened it. She swallowed, trying to relieve her suddenly dry mouth. Patrick looked terrific. He wore a dark business suit, a vivid blue shirt, and a navy-blue necktie. His pale skin clashed with his dark clothing. She twitched her fingers, aching to stroke his short bright red hair. She recalled how they'd spent long evenings together and how she'd loved running her fingers in his thick hair.

He smiled as dimples winked on his pale freckled cheeks. "Good afternoon, Rocky."

His deep hypnotic voice made her swoon. She took a deep breath. "Hi, Patrick. Come on in."

He entered the house. His mouth appeared tense. Oh no. Something was wrong. She touched his arm. "What's the matter?"

He gestured toward the living room. "Could we sit and talk for a minute?"

"Sure."

The blinds were open and buttery bright sunlight splashed into the room. They made themselves comfortable on the couch. He bowed his head and closed his eyes. His lips moved. She assumed he silently prayed. He finally opened his eyes. "Look Rocky. I love you. I shouldn't have kept my mother's suicide a secret from you. I should have asked you to come to Ireland with me but I didn't. I hope you can forgive me. At the time I felt I was making the best decision."

She nodded. She wanted to put him at ease. "Patrick..." She leaned over and kissed him on the cheek. He smelled so good. The woody citrus scent of his Irish cologne opened up a vivid box of memories for her – some memories so vivid...she looked away, her heart suddenly beating hard. She wanted to do more than just kiss Patrick. Again, she recalled what they used to do before they were saved. He caressed her cheek. Her skin warmed beneath his gentle fingers. She focused on his amazing emerald-green eyes. "If the situation were reversed I probably would have done the same."

He took her hand and squeezed it. "Good. I feel better now that I've said that. I also wanted to let you know that I've spoken to my dad. We're going to try to spend more time together as father and son." He took another deep breath. "What you said when we were at the hamburger place, when we had that argument...Rocky...all of it was true. I just wasn't brave enough to admit it to myself. I'm glad you spoke up. I needed to hear that."

Relief, as smooth and rich as golden honey, flowed through her. "I'm so glad you told me that. I was worried that you were mad at me. So, are you still going to work with your dad?"

"No, actually, that's another thing I wanted to tell you. I'm going to take a job as a controller for Fishers of Men Christian School for boys. I won't be working such long hours and the job doubles as an assistant coach position. It'll be nice for me to work with youth again."

Hallelujah! That was a relief. The urge to kiss his beautiful mouth consumed her. She leaned toward him and they kissed. She moaned as he pulled away. His pale skin reddened. Oh no, looked like he was nervous.

"Rocky. I can't be alone with you. I don't trust myself."

Whew she wasn't expecting him to say that. They needed to focus on something else. She took a few deep breaths and stood up. She strolled to the Christmas tree as her heart thundered with pure joy. She took the small wrapped package from beneath the tree. She returned to the couch and set the package on the coffee table. "Merry Christmas."

He grinned as he removed a small package from his pocket. "Merry Christmas."

Warmth flowed through her veins as both of them unwrapped their gifts. "Oh, Patrick. This is lovely." Her voice wavered as she removed the gold charm bracelet. The bracelet had a single cross that dangled from the chain. He helped her to put the bracelet on. She held her wrist up to admire her new gift. Every time she wore this bracelet she would think of Jesus Christ and Patrick. "Thank you."

"Thank you, too." He gestured toward the bottle of Irish cologne that she'd bought for him. It was his favorite scent. She'd had to order it online since it was difficult to find it at stores in the states.

Her heart thundered as they shared a long hug. He smelled so delicious...she just wanted to kiss him again.

Before she could manage to say anything he ended their hug and pulled out his phone and quickly sent a text. A few seconds later a hard knock resonated from the front door. Shocking when Patrick stood up. "I've got this." He opened the door and his father strolled into the room. He didn't appear as uptight as when she met him a few years ago. He looked refreshed – as if he'd gotten a full night's sleep and was ready to have a good time. "Rocky, you remember my dad, Roger Smith, right?"

She finally managed to stand. "So nice to see you again Mr. Smith." She offered her hand, but he pulled her into a hug. After they'd hugged Patrick again took her hand.

"Rocky, my dad agreed to be our chaperone. I don't trust myself to be alone with you."

She laughed and gestured toward the kitchen. "Come on, let's eat."

Six months later...

Raquel slowly walked down the aisle of the church. Her dad, Gregory Montague, slowly limped beside her using his walker. Her and her dad's relationship had strengthened into a strong friendship over the last six months. He'd insisted on walking her down the aisle. Her heart felt warm, toasty, and oh so glad that her earthly father was sharing this day with her. *Lord, thank you so much for giving me the courage and the strength to forgive my father.* Her vivid white gown contrasted with her brown skin. Nervous butterflies exploded in her stomach as they made their way toward the front where Patrick stood – looking handsome and fetching as ever in his tuxedo. She grinned, excited to see the most important man to her on this God-given earth. Melanie, Brooke, Frank's wife Emily, and Patrick's identical twin sisters served as bridesmaids. Their dark purple dresses etched with tiny flowers were the most beautiful bridesmaid dresses she'd ever seen.

Her cousin Frank, Patrick's dad and Patrick's friend and coworker Mr. Evans, and two of Patrick's friends from church served as grooms-men. Their dark purple ties and cummerbunds complemented the bridesmaids' dresses perfectly. Bright white and red roses adorned the church with exquisite sweetness. She briefly glanced at the first row of seats and saw Ama wiping away her tears with a lace-trimmed handkerchief. Ama had been a blessing straight from God. She had a good eye for decorating and planning, so she'd helped Raquel to plan her wedding. During wedding planning Ama had encouraged Raquel to see a therapist about her fear of driving. Slowly, after much time and prayer, she'd signed up for driving lessons. She'd finally gotten her driver's license one month ago. Although she drove, she still feared driving on the highway. She only drove locally. In due time, she might develop the courage, Lord willing, to drive on the interstate. Happy tears welled up in Raquel's eyes as she approached Patrick.

He was definitely the most beautiful man she'd ever seen. She quickly blinked her tears away. No way did she want to risk ruining her makeup.

The pastor stood at the podium and gazed out at the audience. "Who gives this woman away to be with this man?"

"I do." Her father's voice echoed throughout the entire church. A few of the attendees fondly chuckled at his exuberant tone.

After her father had limped back to his seat, the pastor then recited their vows.

"Do you take Raquel to be your lawfully wedded wife?"

Patrick gave her a slow gentle smile. "I do."

"Do you take Patrick to be your lawfully wedded husband?"

"I do."

"I now pronounce you man and wife. You may kiss the bride."

He leaned toward her and their lips locked. The joining of their mouths, soft and gentle, was like a clean cleansing rain on parched earth. So refreshing, so familiar, so loving. "I love you, Rocky." His strong, yet gentle voice, whispered the words in her ear.

She then placed her mouth near his ear. "I love you too, Patrick." She whispered the sweet words right before they shared another kiss.

Thank you for reading Butterscotch Bliss. I hope you loved Patrick and Raquel as much as I do. Rocky Road Dreams — the story that occurs simultaneously with Butterscotch Bliss - delves deeper into the mysterious lives of Melanie and Kyle! Join them on a bizarre road trip as Kyle discovers secrets about his parentage! Order now!

https://ceceliadowdy.com/rocky-road-dreams-lp/

Read the entire series! Download today!

https://ceceliadowdy.com/the-candy-beach-series2/

About Cecelia Dowdy

CECELIA DOWDY is an Amazon bestselling author who lives near Washington DC. She enjoys listening to old tunes with her husband and chauffeuring her teenaged son to his school sports events. Baking is one of her favorite passions. She loves experimenting with bread recipes using her sourdough starter. Serving homemade desserts to friends brings her joy. Her love of baking shines in her romance novels. When she's not in the kitchen, or spending time with her family, she's cooking up delicious faith-filled plots. Fans say reading her tasty novels makes them hungry. Sign up for her newsletter. https://ceceliadowdy.com/sign-up-for-my-email-list/

Connect with Cecelia Dowdy

Join my mailing list! I will keep you updated about future releases: https://ceceliadowdy.com/sign-up-for-my-email-list/

Let's discuss the Bible – visit my Sunday Brunch biblical discussions on my blog:

http://ceceliadowdy.com/blog/category/sunday-brunch

Please visit my website for more of my books:

www.ceceliadowdy.com/

You can also find me on social media (as Cecelia Dowdy or cdnovelist):

Other Titles By Cecelia Dowdy

THE BAKERY ROMANCE SERIES

Loving Luke *(Book 0)*

Raspberry Kisses *(Book 1)*

Shades of Chocolate *(Book 2)*

Sweet Dreams *(Book 3)*

Sugar and Spice *(Book 4)*

Southern Comfort *(Book 5)*

Sweet Delights *(Book 6)*

Cinnamon Kisses *(Book 7)*

THE CANDY BEACH SERIES

https://ceceliadowdy.com/the-candy-beach-series2/

Caramel Kisses – *(Book 0)*

Chocolate Dreams – *(Book 1)*

Milk Chocolate Kisses – *(Book 2)*

Bittersweet Dreams – *(Book 3)*

Coffee and Kisses – *(Book 4)*

Rocky Road Dreams – *(Book 5)*

THE ROMANCE BRIDE SERIES

https://ceceliadowdy.com/romance-bride-series/

The Baker's Bride (an Underground Railroad romance novella) – (Book 1)

The Doctor's Bride (a historical romance novella) – (Book 2)

www.ingramcontent.com/pod-product-compliance
Lightning Source LLC
Chambersburg PA
CBHW070425310726
48977CB00003B/841